REPORTED MISSING

Diane Harding

First ebook edition: Sydney 2016

Publisher: Sydney School of Arts & Humanities

15-17 Argyle Place Millers Point NSW 2000

www.ssoa.com.au

Reported Missing

ISBN: 978-0-9945441-0-0

Cover design by Ferdinando Manzo. Text design by Ferdinando Manzo. Typeset in Times New Roman. Printed and bound by Lightning Source as a POD paperback.

National Library of Australia Cataloguing-in-Publication data:

Harding, Diane, author.

Reported Missing / Diane Harding.

978-0-9945441-2-4

Fiction – domestic violence – crime fiction – Sydney novel – Australian fiction

Dedication

For Rex – with love

Acknowledgements

Without a doubt this work of fiction, my first novel, would not have been published without the encouragement, positive support, brilliant feedback and attention to detail in the editing by the Director of Sydney School of Arts & Humanities (SSOA), Dr Christine Williams, and her team: in particular, Ferdinando Manzo for cover design and formatting and Sharon Dean for proof reading. I would also like to thank my creative writing group for their enthusiasm and positive critiques when I began this endeavour.

Author biography

Diane Harding has worked in education as a primary school teacher, a coordinator for family day care and a writer of text books for TAFE and university.

Chair of the International Family Day Care Organisation for three years, she travelled the world lecturing, then was seconded by the Federal Government to introduce new child care accountability measures across Australia.

Later, she trained workers in legislation covering child abuse.
Now retired in Sydney with her husband, Harding revels in the joy of her grandchildren, Jeremy, Charlotte and Annika.

REPORTED MISSING is her first novel.

Chapter 1

I wasn't suspicious at first when I couldn't make contact with our daughter, Jenny. I just thought it was Jenny being her busy self as usual.

But somehow, and I don't know why, after the third call I began to feel uneasy. Why that was, I couldn't say. After all, I often called her and received no answer, or she did not return my call for a few days. But this time was different.

It was only on the third call to her mobile that I heard John's voice message:

'Jenny's phone is being disconnected at the end of the week and all business calls should be directed to my phone at 4041 942 8374'.

I thought back to the last conversation I'd had with Jenny. Had she mentioned that she was disconnecting her phone? Surely she would have mentioned it. The last time we'd talked had been about preparing an event for her birthday due in a fortnight. We'd chatted about the rental property they were moving to and I had forgotten to get the address and new phone numbers.

Now I didn't know where they lived. I couldn't find her.

My mind went into panic mode. This was my daughter, my lovely bubbly thirty-year-old Jenny – and her husband and two wonderful children – and I didn't know where they all were.

For a moment the world was spinning out of my control. Then

I pulled myself together and told my mind to stop worrying and being silly.

I decided I'd phone John on the work number he'd provided on his phone message. But first I talked with my husband of thirty-seven years just as I always shared any worries over our daughter and her family.

'Mac, I can't get Jenny. Her phone has been disconnected.'

Mac stood in the kitchen doorway. 'Well, phone John then and get the new number,' he said.

'Hmmm. You know what he said last time I phoned him at work. He was so cross.'

'Just do it, Lilli. Forget about his crossness and just do it.'

I picked up the phone and dialled.

Immediately I was connected to an administrative assistant who asked politely how she could help me.

'I'm after John, John Stanford. Can you put me through to him?'

There was a pause before she said, 'I don't have him on my list of personnel here. You must have the wrong number.'

I was flabbergasted. 'This is the number he has given me,' I said. I could hear the whine in my voice.

'Sorry,' she answered. 'But he doesn't work here.'

I put the phone down in its cradle with a bang and yelled out to Mac. 'Guess what? He doesn't work there, if he ever did.'

Life had changed for me the previous October when I'd arrived to do Jenny's administration books and mind the children, who were aged just two and four and a half. This was my three-day-a-week job which I did for free, to help her with her swim school business.

Of course I loved being busy and helping out, and I loved minding the children. But I would have been happy not to have to think about quarterly tax and GST, paying staff and balancing the books … so that when, three months before, she'd announced she was selling the swim school and moving to the Blue Mountains, my first thought was, *'No more business work for me!'*

Then I'd noticed that Jenny's eyes were welling up with tears and I'd realised that this was a big move for her. We commiserated together for a while until I got over the shock of it all, and she said, 'I'll miss you.' And then in her baby voice that she'd always used to get what she wanted, she asked whether Mac and I would think of moving to the mountains to live nearby. After all, we'd loved the mountains and spent quite a bit of time there. We had even owned a holiday home for a while in the main mountain town, Katoomba.

I'd rushed home to Mac that evening and told him the story.

Jenny's knee had twisted while she was running and although she'd had an arthroscopy, the knee still gave way sometimes at work. She felt she couldn't run the business with this injury so she'd decided to sell.

She explained that if she didn't have a job, they'd be stretched to pay the mortgage with only one wage coming in. They had always loved the mountains and they wanted to move before Chiara started school the following year. An almost unheard of flat block of land had become available in the mountains with lovely views, so they'd purchased it immediately. They would be renting until the house was built. Jenny was going to act as the owner and builder-manager.

Mac and I talked about how silly they were to leave Sydney as they might never be able to afford to come back again, what with the rising prices of houses. When I broached the subject of selling and going up there too, Mac said I was too emotional about it all to think straight. We had all our friends here and our social lives and our son and daughter-in-law lived nearby. What would it be like for him if we showed a preference for one child over the other?

I calmed down then and started to examine the idea sensibly.

We loved where we lived on Sydney's northern beaches. Although I'd miss Chiara and Ryan, I could visit them weekly. Time would go by quickly and soon they'd both be at school. Then they'd be busy with friends and I would have them come to stay in the school holidays.

Suddenly it didn't seem so bad. At least I wouldn't have to do the business books ever again. Mac and I had a life to lead too.

Mac was a much more sensible person than I was. I had met him when we were at university together. A crowd of us had formed into a small group that met for coffee and debate after class. Mac was always called Mac as his name was Stanley Ambrose McGregor. I still call him Mac unless I'm very cross. Then I call him Stanley Ambrose.

Back then in those Uni days, after a couple of months we'd begun going out on dates and I discovered that we thought alike about many things and enjoyed laughing together about most things. My dad had always said that if you find someone who you can laugh with, then you're on the way to finding a lifelong companion. A wise man, my father.

Soon our group accepted that we were 'an item', as they said in those days. Our names began to be linked together. 'Let's invite Mac and Lilli,' they'd say, or 'What do Mac and Lilli think?'

Both of us liked walking and spent lots of time outdoors. Mac was also in the local rugby football team in those days and I would go to watch his games, although I often didn't know who was who on the field so I missed some of Mac's best tries. Luckily, he was tolerant when he'd ask if I'd seen his try and I'd confess that I hadn't. Now, after all these years, Mac was still the tolerant one.

After my surprise phone call about the mystery of where John worked, I resolved to go hunting. I searched my mind for any information about the rental that Jenny and the children were going to.

I remembered that she'd told me a suitable place had been hard for them to find in time for the move from their old home. The new owners had given them two months to move out which was quite generous, and now they had to go. The fall-back position was that they would stay with us and commute to the mountains to organise the build and start Chiara in school. But we all felt this would present quite a lot of difficulties for all of us.

Luckily, after denying they had a dog and almost denying they had two children, they were eventually offered a rental that suited. I could remember Jenny saying that it was in Blaxland and it was one half of a duplex, but that was all.

I began to worry.

Why can't I get her on the phone? I've left dozens of messages. She's never this long phoning back even if she's forgotten to look at her messages, or if the mobile's battery is flat. It's been five days. Where is she?

Of course, Mac thought I was paranoid.

'Stop worrying. She'll get back to you and probably say she lost her phone or the kids were playing with it or something like that.' And he turned up the sound on the DVD he was watching.

So I tried to stop thinking about the situation, but it kept creeping back into my mind. It felt like the times when Jenny was little and had hidden amongst the dresses in Warringah Mall, and for a minute there I couldn't find her.

She's my child still and I need to hear her voice, I persuaded myself. I don't need to be stressed like this.

So in desperation, I phoned John on the message machine number again.

This time there was a pause and a click as if the phone was being redirected. John answered with his business tone of voice.

'John, it's Lilli. I tried to phone this number before but they said you didn't work there. Thank goodness I've found you at last. Sorry I'm phoning you at work as I know you don't like personal calls, but I can't seem to get onto Jenny and hoped you could give her a message for me, or, if she has a new phone, you could give me the number.'

I was pretty breathless after this long explanation.

'I don't know where she is,' he said, and I could hear the change from business tone to frigidity in his voice.

'What, what did you say?' I stuttered, although I'd heard perfectly well what he'd said.

'Just what I said,' he spat down the phone line. 'She's left me, so don't phone again,' he said and hung up.

Chapter 2

Now I was worried.

Where would Jenny go if she had left John? It seemed to me that her first port of call would be us, her mum and dad. We would be the obvious ones to offer her comfort, support and beds for her and the children. Where else would she go with her two little ones?

I thought about my two lovely grandchildren. Ryan, aged two, a cheeky, constantly laughing boy, with curly hair that fell over his forehead in a riotous tangle of red. And Chiara, a lanky nearly-five year old with blue sparkly eyes full of curiosity, and an interest in stories and reading, even though she wasn't yet at school.

I worried about them all night, getting up at least three or four times and disturbing Mac as I did.

'Stop worrying and get back to sleep, Lilli,' was all he could mutter. But still I went over and over John's words in my mind.

Then I thought of our son, Tony. Perhaps she'd gone to him. Brothers and sisters often told each other things that they couldn't tell their parents. I decided I'd phone Tony at his work. Even though tomorrow was Saturday, he worked at the business six days a week.

When I called him the next morning, he answered in his professional voice and asked how he could be of help.

'Hi Tony,' I said.

'Hey,' he replied. 'Nice to hear from you, Mum. But you never phone me at work. Is something wrong? Is Dad all right? Are you?'

I could hear the concern in his voice and knew without a doubt that he was not hiding anything from me about Jenny.

'I'm just checking on whether you've seen or heard from Jenny recently.'

'No, Mum, not since our last family dinner. Why?'

I told him the story of trying to call her and then talking to John.

'Poor Jenny. Where is she now?'

'I don't know', I wailed. 'I thought she might have come to you for help or at least spoken to you.'

'No, I haven't heard a thing. I'll phone John and see what else I can find out. I'll get back to you asap.'

He hung up and I just sat by the phone with nothing to do but worry about my daughter.

Jenny had always had two very good friends, Annika and Callie. They had been friends since infants school. The three of them used to walk to school together as we and their parents all lived in adjacent streets. As teenagers, they'd giggled over boyfriends. They'd been bridesmaids at each other's weddings. Perhaps Jenny had gone to them for help. After all, they had children too and would give her children a stable and happy change, almost like a holiday without the drama of seeing their parents separating. I went straight to the online directory and found both the girls' mothers' numbers because I couldn't remember their married names.

What could I say? I didn't want to confess that I didn't know my own daughter's number. I didn't want to say she'd left her husband and I didn't know where she was.

Finally I decided what to say.

'Hi, this is Jenny's mother here. I'm trying to contact Jenny at your daughter's place and Jenny's phone is dead. Could I have your daughter's number? It's a bit of an emergency as her aunt is very ill.'

Both the girls' mothers were kind of old-time friends as we'd had quite a lot of contact while they were growing up, so they were willing to give me the numbers. Then came the next difficult task of asking Jenny's friends if she was there. Again, I worked out an explanation for my call that sounded plausible.

'Hello, Annika? It's Jenny's mother here. I've just had news that Jenny's aunt is very ill and I'm trying to contact her. Of course her phone would be dead at this time and I thought she was visiting you. Could I speak to her please?'

'Oh, Mrs McGregor, she's not here. I haven't heard from her for a while as we've only just come back from a holiday in Fiji. In fact, I haven't heard from her in two months. Not since our daughter's birthday party in April. But if I hear from her, I'll let her know you called.'

Then I tried Callie with the same weak explanation. Her husband answered the phone and when he heard my story his reply was,

'Sorry Mrs McGregor, but Callie has been in hospital for the past two weeks with a severely broken leg. You're just lucky you got me, as the kids and I have been living at my mother's place in Sutherland, and I just came home to get a few clothes and toys for them. Sorry, but I can't help you.'

So I couldn't do anything more until I heard from Tony.

Just then the phone rang and I snatched it up with a reflex action that was so fast I dropped it and had to catch the swinging cord.

'Mum,' Tony said, 'I rang John but he was very angry and hardly spoke to me. I was only able to find out that Jenny left two weeks ago and took the children with her. She didn't say where she was going. Just got in the car and went. Mum, I got a bit cross then and asked him what he'd done to make her leave, and added that if he'd been abusing my sister I'd be round there to knock his block off. He didn't take kindly to what I said, but answered that he hadn't done anything like that. He said he loved Jenny and wanted her back, and his kids back too. I believe him, Mum. He sounded very distraught to me.'

Two weeks ago! I was shocked.

'Where is she then? I've phoned her friends Annika and Callie but they haven't seen her. What's happening, Tony? Something's wrong I know it.' I could hear the fretting tone in my voice.

'Hey, Mum. It's okay. You'll see. She was probably so upset that she went off to recover on her own. She'll contact you soon. Go talk to Dad about it. He'll have some ideas about what to do.'

And with that Tony was off. 'Got to go, Mum – the office is calling. Phone me with any news,' he said before abruptly hanging up.

Tony didn't seem to be worried. I was becoming frustrated with people who didn't think the situation was strange.

I almost ran down the hall from the kitchen to the lounge room where Mac was flicking through TV channels. He'd been at a bit of a loss since he'd retired three years ago and was starting to watch soaps and reality shows during the day.

I filled him in on everything I'd done and everything the people I'd contacted had said. It was beginning to sound more shocking to me as I explained it. Where would she go with two children aged nearly five and two?

What could have made her leave? Has she been hurt and can't contact anyone? Has John thought of this possibility? Has he phoned the police? I can't leave it like this.

Even though he'd expressly said not to phone him, I decided that was what I needed to do.

Thank goodness it was a Saturday and I could phone him on his mobile at home. He might be more amenable at answering questions when he was not at work.

I punched in the numbers and waited through a few bars of *Lord of the Rings* before I heard his voice.

'John, it's just me again, Lilli. I was so shocked to hear Jenny had left that I forgot to ask you some questions. Did you see her leave? She hasn't contacted us. Could something have happened to her? Have you phoned the police?'

I could hear John taking a deep breath before he answered me.

'No, Lilli, nothing has happened to her and I haven't phoned the police because she's not missing or in danger. She left me a note to say she was leaving because she'd found someone else. She's taken all her clothes and the children's clothes and left without a forwarding address or phone number. I don't want to talk about it and I don't want you interfering. I just want to be left alone.'

I suddenly felt sorry for the man. It seemed that my daughter was wrong this time. It was a terrible thing to do. It was not the way we'd brought her up at all.

I was slowly putting the phone down on the hook when I heard a voice in the background saying, 'Nanna, Nanna,' and then the connection was broken.

What did I really hear, I asked myself. Was it just wishful thinking that I heard a child's voice? Was it just the dog whining or the sound of wind in the background, or even John crying on the other end of the phone?

I tried to recapture the moment, and finally decided that, yes, that voice had been Ryan's. It had the same inflection that two year olds often have when they're learning to speak. It simply sounded like Ryan to me, not another two-year-old – and I knew his voice very well. Minding him three days a week for almost nine months, I knew his voice as well as I'd known my own children's when they were young.

That meant that the children were there with John! It also meant that Jenny must be there, because she would never leave her children – unless something had happened to her.

And if that was the case, John was lying.

Chapter 3

John …! I thought about John. *Why would he lie to me?*

Eleven years ago Jenny was in love. She had brought home this guy she'd met at university while she was studying teaching. Mac, of course, was very suspicious of anyone who was interested in his only daughter, and didn't like him at first. But we could see that he was a confident young man with lots of opinions and an ability to converse on any subject.

He was well-built, rather handsome in the way that young people of the day liked, tall, lithe, with wavy brown hair, long at the back, a stubble of whiskers, and a great smile.

Also, he was from England with a rather posh accent and an overseas past that remained quite mysterious to us Aussies. Yes, Mac wasn't happy that Jenny had an Englishman as a boyfriend at first because, being a history buff, he didn't like the way the 'Poms' had treated Australians in World War I and II. But as we got to know John we could see why he would appeal to Jenny. He was so attentive to her, obviously adored her, and was a good provider, easily able to get well-paid jobs.

The only real concern we had about him was a lack of relatives and friends at the wedding. We wondered why, but then thought that he'd probably had to leave old friends behind in making a new life here in Australia.

It was only after a year or two that we began to see the other side of John. He was a bragger, and occasionally a liar, and seemed to need Jenny's good opinion all the time.

Now I recalled the times he'd seemed to lie to us, or at least tell tall stories. There was the time he was supposedly buying a holiday apartment in the Caribbean which fell through at the last minute, or the time he was getting a raise and being made manager of the company, even though he'd only been there for a few months. Neither of these plans came to pass. And only the other day I'd discovered he didn't work at the office which had the number he'd given me.

I remembered how jealous he would be whenever we visited and took up Jenny's time. I thought about how he used to phone Jenny when she was at our place at least five times a day to see where she was and what she was doing. In fact, all the bad things I knew about my son-in-law kept nudging out any sensible thoughts in my mind.

What should I do?

I decided to take things into my own hands. Mac still wasn't convinced that John was playing a devious role. But he'd obviously decided that I needed to get these thoughts out of my system with some positive action.

So we decided that I would drive to Blaxland, find their rental home and see if Jenny and the kids were there.

The next day was bright and sunny, which lifted my anxious mood to one of hope and common sense.

A quick look in the full length mirror showed a sixty-year-old woman with greying hair who wasn't in bad shape at all. My brown jeans and layered cream, brown and black silk top with a bright green scarf knotted at my throat made me look respectable and even pretty good, I thought – as if I was going visiting or on holiday, not desperately trying to find my daughter.

I didn't want to appear distressed, so I suggested Mac stay home.

I drove straight up the highway via the M2, the M7 and the M4 to Blaxland. The town in the foothills of this imposing mountain range had once been a small village stretched along the Great Western Highway, but now I realised that it extended into new subdivisions and cul-de-sacs in bushland on either side of the road. So I drove up and down a few of these streets, imagining I might come across a duplex that was theirs. How many duplexes could there be?

I soon realised that I was wasting my time and energy.

The best option was to visit the three real estate agencies on the main road and ask for the tenants, Jenny and John Stanford.

The first agency I approached had a big rental sign in the window. I felt that it looked promising.

'I'm looking for John and Jenny Stanford who may have rented a duplex in Blaxland from you. Can you tell me if you know them, and where they live?'

'Sorry,' came the reply from a well-dressed receptionist, 'but we can't give out any confidential information about our clients.'

I immediately thanked her and backed quickly out the door feeling such a dummy. I knew how businesses worked. I'd even said the same thing to others who had coming knocking on our business door. What was I thinking?

I would have to be smarter than that to find out anything. Before I entered the next agency, I concocted a story.

'Good morning,' I said in a pleasant tone. 'I still haven't found a rental in Blaxland. I did look at a duplex in the last two weeks. Is it still available? I think it was … um … Can you remind me where it was again?'

'The duplexes have all gone,' the receptionist said sympathetically. 'But I can keep you in mind. What was your name? I'll put a reminder against your name.'

She pressed a button on her computer and waited expectantly for me to give my name.

'Jenny Stanford,' I said.

'Oh dear,' she said. 'It must have been some other agency because you aren't on our list. Would you like me to add your name now? There's a form to fill in, and you can do it right now.'

'Um … No thanks. I'd better find my own agency, I think.' Once again I ducked out the door very quickly.

This was no good, I decided. I'd have to go back to my original idea of driving the streets. Perhaps I needed a more organised and grid-like approach.

I remembered Jenny saying the duplex was new, as well as something else I'd just recalled. I'd asked her if the duplex neighbours would be unhappy when the children were crying or even shouting and screaming in fun. She'd said that the garages for both dwellings were in the middle, so the noise would be even less than for the neighbours on the other side around the corner.

A corner. That's the key to the puzzle. I'll look for duplexes on street corners.

So I began at the end of the village, driving up one new subdivision after another on the left-hand-side. Fortunately the subdivisions were small, with the land they occupied dropping away to cliffs.

I'd been up the left-hand-side of one street, had turned around at the end of the village, and was slowly coming down the right-hand-side when I entered a small cul-de-sac with a dogleg corner about halfway down the street. There at the end of the turning circle was a duplex building with two garages in the centre. The next-door neighbour was just around the corner as well.

This could be it, I thought. I was shaking with excitement.

I parked on the blind side of the dogleg corner to avoid John recognising my car. I didn't want him to think I was spying, even if that was what I was doing. Rummaging in the boot, I found one of Mac's fishing hats and a parka. I felt more confident wearing them for disguise. Down the road I walked.

The open garage on the left side duplex was full of boxes, furniture and tools. The car sitting on the driveway had a baby seat and a booster, just what Chiara and Ryan would need.

I didn't recognise the car though. *Could he have bought another car?* I needed to be sure.

I noticed a woman sweeping leaves off her verandah on a big house diagonally opposite the duplex. She was slim with grey hair and a pursed mouth. A busybody, I thought. Just the sort of person who might give me some information. I got out, walked down the driveway, and approached her slowly.

'Hello,' I smiled. 'I'm visiting Jenny and have forgotten which is her duplex. Do you know Jenny Stanford? Do you know which one she's in?'

'Oh yes,' she said, pointing to the left. 'She's had her hands full the last few nights. In fact, Ryan even kept me awake last night with his crying. I bet she's getting no sleep at all.'

'Thanks very much,' I said, and turned towards the house.

I pretended to walk towards it then I clicked my fingers as if I'd forgotten something and turned back towards the car.

'Well, no sound now. I'll just give her a while longer,' I said. 'Every wink of sleep counts.'

The woman nodded.

I'll sit in the car and act as if I'm making a few phone calls while I wait for someone to come out of the house, I thought. I hoped the neighbour was taken in by my acting, that she didn't doubt my excuse and think there was something weird about me hurrying up the road instead of going to the front door. I was so elated I almost skipped up the hill to the car.

About thirty minutes later I saw John come out of the garage. He stood looking up the road in the opposite direction from where I was parked before he drove his car into the small car space between the boxes and furniture in his garage and shut the garage door behind him.

Sliding down behind the steering wheel, I tried not to make any jerky movement that he would notice if he looked my way. Thank goodness I'd kept the hat on my head.

Anger was my overriding feeling now. I was angry that I felt forced to sneak around and be devious. I was angry that they were there and I was being lied to. I was angry with myself because it was getting dark and I was unsure what to do next.

And I had so many questions. *If Jenny is inside, why doesn't she want to see me? Has she made John say she's left? I don't believe it. Is John keeping them all from us? Is his jealousy becoming worse? Does Jenny even know I'm trying to contact her?*

Having patience was the answer, I decided. I'd come back the next day, wait for John to go out, and then I'd knock on the door.

It was too far to go home, so I booked into a motel on the main road for the night and phoned Mac. For the first time I heard anger in his voice as well as confusion. At last he believed me. And there was something very strange about what was going on.

'Power up your phone and keep in touch tomorrow,' he said. 'But Lilli, don't take any risks.'

By six o'clock the next morning, I was showered and dressed in yesterday's clothes. I drove to the same spot where I'd parked before. I walked down the road, already feeling that something was wrong.

The garage door was open and empty. The car was not there.

I stood in the driveway, my arms hanging by my side and my mind empty.

'Yoo-hoo,' called a voice from the next door verandah.

'You just missed them,' said the neighbour. 'They've gone. I saw them packing up last night and they left early this morning.'

'Just John?' I asked hopefully.

'No, John and Jenny and the kids,' she said.

I was too late.

Chapter 4

There was nothing to do but drive home, and so I did.

Mac listened to the whole story and held me close, as I kept saying, 'What if I had gone to the house yesterday?'

He finally convinced me that anything I could have done would have had the same result. They would have left.

So a series of days began where I just went through the motions of living, and in between times, just sitting on the lounge dejected and sad, I would gaze at nothing.

Tony and my daughter-in-law, Samantha, came by to try to cheer me up but I could see they were as worried as I was, and no real help at all.

Samantha sat close and offered tea and sympathy as best she could. She was a lovely daughter-in-law, with a round open face and a disarming smile. Just the sort of wife we thought was right for Tony. But when they left for home in the late afternoon, I was glad to see them leave so I could go back to my own thoughts.

Mac made dinner, which I hardly touched, and I went to bed early. In the middle of the night I woke with a start. Mac was spooned behind me and grunted awake when I turned to him. I had remembered something important. Something I had forgotten.

'Mac, Mac,' I almost yelled, I was so excited.

John worked in the city, I'd remembered, and I'd been to his office before with Jenny, so I knew where the entrance was to his office building. I could go there and follow him home.

It was such a brilliant idea that Mac actually sat up and gazed at me.

'All right, Lilli. We'll do it today.'

Mac and I couldn't go back to sleep, and kept mulling over the idea, until at 6am we were up and dressed.

We had both decided to disguise ourselves. We looked too old to be students and too casual to be workers. So we decided on disguises as tourists. In that way we could have nondescript plain clothes, peaked hats and backpacks with other changes of clothes.

We went online to find the bus timetable for the shopping centre near our home, then paid our $2.50 seniors fare to the city. I set my mind to remembering the route Jenny and I had taken from the carpark to John's office.

Once we'd reached Wynyard, we walked down to Kent St and the couple of blocks to John's building. There was a café across the road, where we sat at bench-like tables facing the window, opposite the building where I thought John worked. I hoped I'd remembered it correctly.

On the other side of the road were several government buildings with large entrances and foyers. People kept coming and going so it was difficult to maintain our vigilance and not let our minds wander off into imaginings. My eyes got tired from staring at everyone, until finally Mac and I decided to take turns at watching.

The café was quite small with just a counter, where you could buy sandwiches and drinks, and three tables with chairs, as well as a bar along the front wall where customers stood or sat on stools. Several people came in during the day and stood near us with their coffees, some with newspapers and many more staring at their mobiles. Fortunately the tables were never full. We'd wondered if we might be thrown out for staying too long if there was a crowd waiting.

We didn't see John go into the building in the morning or come out at lunchtime, and by the afternoon we were tired of buying everything on the menu. I began to despair over whether I had the right building.

Then, just as we were thinking we should try another day, John came out through the sliding doors of the building with his briefcase and a carry-all filled with brightly coloured parcels.

He was surrounded by other 'suits', all clapping him on the back and shaking hands.

'I bet he's just resigned and they've given him presents and a send-off,' I whispered to Mac. 'Look at that parcel peeping out of his carry-all. It has coloured paper and ribbon tied to it.'

A gesture from one of the men seemed to suggest a drink at the pub down the street. John shook his head, shook hands again all round, and strode off in the other direction.

Quickly, Mac and I jumped up, left two twenty dollar notes on the table, and raced out the café door.

We skittered along on the other side of the road from John, keep-ing back just enough not to lose sight of him.

'He's going to Wynyard station,' I puffed. 'We'll have to get clos-er or we'll lose him.'

We ran across the road when we saw a break in the traffic and wove in and out of a crowd of business people hurrying for the station and home. John strode into the entrance to Wynyard station and hurried to the long elevator. We raced to it too, hoping like crazy that he wouldn't look back.

He didn't.

On the escalator, we partially hid behind two taller men but our eyes were trained on the figure of John. Fortunately he was 188 centimetres tall and had a long black business coat, with a distinctive maroon scarf tossed about his neck.

'Mac,' I squeaked. 'He's probably got a weekly pass and we have no tickets to the mountains for the automatic turnstile. Can you go get tickets while I try to follow him? Keep your mobile on so I can tell you where I am.'

Mac disappeared to the left towards the ticket dispensers at the bottom of the elevator, while I followed John to the automatic turnstiles on the right. There was a row of five turnstiles. Commuters put their tickets in, the barrier would open, and they collected their tickets when they popped up at the other end of the turnstile. I couldn't climb over the barrier and I couldn't crawl under it.

At the end of the row of turnstiles was a ticket collector at a gate for people in wheelchairs or with prams, who couldn't negotiate the turnstiles.

I ran up to him, panting, and said, 'There's a man ... I think he's had a stroke. He's lying on the ground.' I waved vaguely behind me.

The ticket collector peered in the direction I'd pointed and after staring at me for a moment and possibly deciding I was a nice person and wouldn't lie, he eventually set off to investigate.

I ran through the gap and down the stairs onto the platform below. Platform 2 went to the city circle. Platform 1 went to Central.

If John was going home to a new place close to the rental he'd been in, he would have to go to Central and then on to the Blue Mountains. I crossed my fingers that he hadn't come back to Sydney with the family and I had chosen the right platform.

So, keeping close to the back wall and moving from one group of commuters to another, I threaded my way down the platform searching for John.

There he was. Huddled with a group who obviously knew where the doors of the train would open when it arrived.

'Mac,' I whispered into my mobile. 'I've got him. I'm on Platform 1. Where are you?'

'Right behind you, Lilli,' Mac whispered back. I turned to see him threading his way towards me and staring beyond my shoulder at John.

'Don't look at his face,' I hissed. 'I've heard that people can sense when they are being stared at and will turn towards you. We don't want that.'

A sudden draft of cold air hit the platform and we knew the train was coming.

The noise from the tunnel grew louder and everyone strained forward. I was concerned that John would get on and we would lose him in the crush. I scrambled forward with everyone else and jumped onto the open section. Mac moved up behind me and we stood together, turning away from the doorway and holding a pole near the entrance to the seating section.

'Mac,' I said. 'We don't know where he'll get off. If it's Springwood, Leura or Katoomba we know that there'll be a fair number of commuters getting off as well, so we can hide in the crowd. But what if he gets off at one of the smaller stations where there are only four or five people leaving? We'll be seen.'

We were both anxious at the thought. Luckily for us, a slashing rain started as we passed through Penrith.

'Let's put on our raincoats and hoods and you can put up your umbrella as well when we get off,' Mac suggested.

We waited as the train passed through Springwood and at last stopped at Leura where John stepped onto the platform. We had to quickly lower our heads so that he wouldn't see us.

'Quick,' I said. 'Get off now.' We huddled in our raingear and waited until John started up the stairs from the platform. He was jogging up two and three stairs at a time.

Mac and I tried to keep up. We hung onto the rail when we could but often had to run around groups that were chatting as they walked. We're getting too old for this, I thought. I could see John walking across the bridge to the stairs that led down to the outside carpark. Mac and I were puffing, but we put on a burst of speed and just hoped that John wouldn't turn around and spot us.

We got to the bridge and started down the outside stairs. Mac got to the bottom first. I could see John further down the street, unlocking his motorbike from the all-day stand and revving the motor. Then he set off over the road bridge and down Leura's main street.

I turned to Mac to point out that John had driven straight ahead rather than turn left or right at the roundabout, when I noticed Mac's colour and his stance. Suddenly he crumpled to the ground and lay still. His breath was coming in loud rasping pants and he seemed unconscious.

A man who'd just reached the last step called out to the gathering crowd, 'Heart attack! Quick, someone, phone for an ambulance.'

Oh no, my Mac. I knelt by him. He was breathing so he didn't need CPR. I struggled to turn him onto the side position.

The helpful man then knelt beside me and assisted me in turning him.

'Thank you so much,' I said. 'Thanks for your help.'

It was only a few minutes before the ambulance arrived and I stepped back to allow the paramedics to do their job. Then I scrambled into the ambulance to ride along with Mac, looking back to say one last, 'Thank you,' to the helpful man, still looking on.

In no time at all we would reach Katoomba Hospital, only five kilometres away.

The paramedics worked on Mac in the ambulance. One applied an oxygen mask to Mac's mouth and the other inserted life-giving tubes into his arm. When we arrived at Casualty, I walked alongside the trolley, holding Mac's hand, while the paramedics walked on the other side. Then I had to release his hand as they took him into the emergency section while I filled in admission papers and sat on a chair in the waiting room.

It was all too much. First our daughter was missing and now Mac had had a heart attack and might not recover.

I burst into noisy sobs. The half dozen people in the waiting room turned to look at me sympathetically for a few moments, and then went back to thinking about their own pain and distress. I was alone.

A half hour later a doctor came out and called my name. He seemed to be smiling. Was this his normal helpful doctor-look even when he was about to give bad news? My ears were filled with white noise and I couldn't hear what he was saying. I guess he could sense I was not really hearing him, so he put his hand on my shoulder and repeated it. This time I heard.

'Your husband is lucky. It was extremely high blood pressure which made it difficult for him to breathe and caused his unconscious state. He has avoided a serious stroke or heart attack. He's okay. But we'll keep him in tonight and possibly tomorrow. It all depends how quickly we can get his blood pressure down to normal. You can come in and see him now.'

I sat by the bed holding Mac's hand. He was still breathing heavily and seemed to be almost asleep.

'He's just had some medicine to calm him down, love,' said the nurse who'd bustled into the room. 'He'll be asleep soon. You can stay for a short while, then I suggest you go home. Leave your phone number at the nurses' station just in case.'

Just in case of what? I thought. I had heard that patients liked to be talked to even if they didn't want to, or couldn't, respond. So I rested my head on my arms and talked softly of how we had met and all the good times we'd had together over the years.

We'd yearned to travel. Mac was a history buff with a degree in ancient history, which later led to his becoming a teacher. I was just a person who wanted to go everywhere and see everything. Once our degrees were completed, we'd set off on a world tour, as kids from Australia did back in the '70s. We did it the hard way with not much money, just walking shoes, a map and a backpack.

I remembered the day Mac had asked me to marry him, he'd said, 'Lilli Walters will you marry me?' Straight off the bat, I'd replied, 'All my life I've been looking for someone whose name doesn't start with a "W" because I'm always the last to be picked for anything, and today I've found you. A name starting with "M" is a good step up for me. So, yes, yes, yes.'

He'd laughed as he wrapped his arms around me; we kissed and were as happy as it was possible to be.

Tears flowed down my cheeks as I thought about our lives together. I didn't want to lose him.

By 8pm when the nurse came back in, I was ready to go.

As I murmured softly to Mac, I devised a plan of action. I would phone the Carrington Hotel, book a room, a seat in the dining room for dinner and breakfast and a car for tomorrow. I phoned for a taxi straight away.

The driver took me around the circular drive at The Carrington to the marble stairs leading up the front of the building.

The Carrington Hotel was a beautiful 1920s building with art deco finishes. The prize of Katoomba in its heyday, it fell into disrepair in the 1970s when holidaymakers discovered the wonders of overseas ship and air travel. The hotel had closed its doors and remained closed for years until an enterprising company put up the cash for repairs to comply with new fire safety regulations. It was now open to the public, offering plush dining rooms, bars and lounges as well as luxurious accommodation.

As I undressed and sat on the bed, I thought about how in our youth Mac and I had envisaged a time when we would have enough money to stay here. And now here I was alone, without Mac to share the enjoyment.

I lay back exhausted and closed my eyes.

Chapter 5

The next morning, after phoning the hospital to see how Mac was, I had breakfast in the dining room. After a delicious spread that I couldn't really appreciate, I spoke to the reception about one more night's accommodation and then walked a few doors down the main street to pick up my rental car.

Thank goodness it was Avis, which meant that I could drive to Sydney when Mac was ready to go home and return the car to the rental company there.

I had a restless night, waking up several times, worried about Mac and about what to do, knowing that John, Jenny and the children were in Leura.

I was thinking that John and Jenny didn't have any friends up this way that I knew of, so it was likely that they were staying in rented premises or a hotel. Then I remembered that they'd come to a Leura B&B for their honeymoon, and had kept coming back for a celebratory weekend every year since. I didn't know where it was but had heard Jenny say that the name of the place reminded her of her grandparents' holiday home.

Mac was awake and sitting up when I arrived at the hospital. His colour was normal and he was smiling. I gave him a big hug.

'You look okay,' I told him, even though he didn't look his best.

'I feel it too. I guess you always feel better when your doctor says it was blood pressure and not a heart attack. I'm sorry we lost John though.'

'Forget it. Your health is more important than losing John. But I do have an idea to follow as soon as they release you from here.'

For the next two days Mac and I discussed my idea. He, sitting up in bed and grumbling about the food, while I walked the floor and thought out loud.

On the second day of his stay, I went to the tourist information office. The walls were covered with pictures of some of the sights that were attractions on the mountains – the Scenic Railway, Jenolan Caves, Govetts Leap and the Three Sisters.

On the counter were brochures of every kind. I looked for a section on accommodation and eventually went up to the counter to ask for a list of all the B&Bs in Leura.

A jolly, round-faced, fifty-something woman behind the counter printed out a two-page list of names and addresses.

I scanned the list quickly, hoping that I would see something that reminded me of my parents' place.

There it was.

'Silver Gums'. The name my parents, now passed away, had given their holiday home. They had built their entrance gates between two lovely spreading gums in the front garden.

Surely this was it.

I returned to the counter to try to find out more.

'I'm quite interested in this one. Do you have a map of where it is?'

'Yes,' said the jolly woman. 'Would you like me to phone them to see if they have a vacancy?'

'No. I'd rather just drive by and see if I like the look of it first, if that's okay.'

She slid a copy of a Leura map onto the counter and traced a line from the tourist bureau to the B&B. It wasn't far.

Buoyed up with hope, I drove back to the hospital to Mac.

'The doctor says my blood pressure is back to normal and I can leave as soon as I like. We have to go to the chemist downstairs first and have this script filled for tablets. Looks like I'll be on them for life now,' he groaned.

I hugged him in sympathy and started to gather his things as he dressed to leave.

The doctor breezed in. 'Give up running up and down stairs for a while,' he quipped. 'And see your own doctor for the next four weeks until your blood pressure has settled.'

He handed a letter to Mac for his regular doctor, shook hands and breezed out again.

At last we were on our way. I drove while Mac examined the map and directed us to the street.

It was a pleasant street with a few older homes and some very nice Federation-style houses surrounded by attractive old-fashioned gardens.

'Silver Gums' was about halfway down the street, next to a small park. It had a wrought iron sign painted in silver on the gate. I drove past it and parked about three houses down, in a generous space between two cars. We'd taken the precaution of wearing our hat and scarf disguises but I felt confident that the hire car would also be a good foil. We stared at each other with delight.

On the road out the front of 'Silver Gums' was a car that looked like the one I'd seen in the garage in Blaxland, with a baby seat and booster in it. Parked in front of it was a motorbike that looked like the bike John had been riding.

We sat in the car and I glanced again at Mac's face. I didn't want him to have another bout of high blood pressure.

Just then, John strode out of the gate, wearing jeans and a long-sleeved casual shirt. He slid into the driver's side and started the car. Obviously he was going out. Hooray!

We waited until he had completed a U-turn, driven up to the corner and turned right towards the Leura shops.

'Come on,' I yelled. 'Now's our chance.'

'Lilli, wait,' Mac said. 'You go up and knock on the door. I'll drive to the corner and keep an eye out for him returning. By the way he was dressed he looked as if he may only have gone out for milk or a paper. Those weren't work clothes. Keep your mobile handy so I can phone you if I see him coming back.'

I slammed the car door and raced to the 'Silver Gums' gate while Mac moved, all stiff limbs, over into the driver's seat.

The house, set back from the road, had two entrances. The front entrance looked like the original main entrance with a portico over an oak door. The second entrance was at the side of the house towards the back. A sign with an arrow indicated an entrance to '3B'. The side door had a path to the small park next door that seemed to extend through to the next block.

I recognised that '3B' would most likely be the B&B entrance and knocked on the door.

In just a few seconds that felt more like ten minutes as I fidgeted on the step, the door was opened by Jenny.

I almost fell over the doorstep and into her arms, crying and smiling at the same time.

'Mum,' she sighed, great relief showing in her expression. 'Quick, come into the kitchenette and shut the door so the children don't see you. How did you find me? I've despaired of ever seeing you again.'

I looked at Jenny properly now and saw her thin worried face, a black eye and swollen jaw. Tears sparkled in her eyes.

'What happened? Tell me.'

'John has changed. He's strange. He's taken away my car keys, my credit cards, my passport, my mobile phone and changed the bank accounts so only he can draw down cash. He's left his job and has started organising passports and tickets to New Zealand. We moved here from Blaxland the other day. He said he didn't want anyone interfering with us again and if I contacted anyone he would take the children away and disappear forever. He could, too. There's nothing I can do. Nothing.'

She held on to me tightly. 'I don't want the kids to see you. Chiara would tell John as soon as he came home. And he might take them away.'

Jenny burst into tears and I wrapped my arms around her, murmuring words of comfort.

I swiftly made up my mind to fix it now.

'Get the kids and come with me. Don't take anything with you. Just come.'

'But what about our clothes and things?'

'Nothing,' I said. 'Come now.'

Jenny went to the lounge area where the kids were watching a DVD.

They ran to me and I hugged them with one arm while I redialled Mac.

'Quick, Mac, I've found Jenny. Go around the block to the park. I can see it runs through to the next street. Just wait there for us. But phone if you see John coming past the end of the street. I'm bringing Jenny and the kids with us.'

I turned to the children. 'Okay, you two, let's go on a surprise hunt for dinosaurs. Come on, run to the park gate. Let's go. As fast as we can.'

I grabbed Chiara's hand, Jenny picked up Ryan, and we ran to the side gate. Once into the park we turned towards the fence along the back where I could see another gate leading out into the back street. Just then my phone rang. 'Yes,' I breathed, scrabbling for my phone, still holding Chiara's hand.

'He's just turned into the street. I was well hidden and I don't think he saw me,' Mac said. 'Hurry, Lilli, hurry.'

We ran through the gate and by this time I was almost dragging Chiara along.

Mac was just outside with the motor running. I opened the back door and shoved Chiara in, with Jenny and Ryan tumbling in behind her. I jumped into the front seat and commanded them, 'Get down on the floor. Hide. Quickly!'

The kids must have abandoned any hope of a dinosaur adventure.

Then Mac was off, foot flat to the accelerator. When he reached the corner he turned right towards the main Leura shops, keeping up the pace. At the roundabout we saw a sign to Sydney. There was nowhere else to go but home. Mac turned right and sped off. I'd look back every few minutes hoping we hadn't been discovered and that we weren't being followed, while two little faces and one scared adult face looked up at me from the floor of the back seat.

Chapter 6

When I felt it was safe for the children and Jenny to sit up on the seats, Jenny snapped on their seat belts.

I wanted her to tell us what had happened in detail, but felt that with the children listening, it wasn't the time. So we began to talk about what to do next.

'We can't just go home. It isn't safe. He's sure to come to our house to check whether you're there …' Mac began.

'Who are you talking about?' piped up our curious four-year-old Chiara from the back seat.

'Nobody you would know,' I said, reminded not to use John's name when little ears were listening to every word.

'You're right, Mac,' I said. 'We need to find a safe place.'

'It can't be Tony's house or even some of Jenny's best friends. In fact …' I turned to Jenny, 'you've probably left your address book at Leura, so he could find your friends easily.'

Jenny sighed again. 'It can't be a motel. The children would never last in one room.'

I immediately thought of a friend of ours.

'What about Wolf's house. He's away for four months and the place is empty. We've always thought it looked like a fortress.'

Wolfgang Ruger was a German friend of ours who regularly went back to Germany each year. It just so happened that he'd left the previous week, after we'd popped over to his house for a coffee while he ran through the security procedures with us again, and gave us his keys and contact numbers.

His house was a two-storey brick place in Belrose, a few suburbs away from us. It had a brick, six foot fence around it with a remote-controlled driveway gate. With another small gate for pedestrian entry, opened with a key, it was just the place for Jenny and the children to stay until this bizarre situation was resolved.

Mac said he'd phone Wolf for his permission, even though he was sure there'd be no problem.

'I'll also ask him to phone his two neighbours to tell them there'll be someone staying in the house, just in case they phone the police thinking there are burglars.'

We swapped drivers so that Mac could phone Wolf straight away. We were lucky he was there as it was around 6am in Berlin. After a short explanation we obtained Wolf's permission.

'We need to stop off at Warriewood Square and get some basic clothes for the three of you, some food and two prepaid disposable phones. That should cut off all phone communication between you and him. You don't need any emotional pressure,' I said.

Jenny readily agreed.

I leaned over to Mac. 'We need to be quick. I reckon John would have looked around the street, and then up towards the shops and maybe the railway station. Then he would suspect us because of the incident at Blaxland – we'd be the most obvious rescuers.'

I still didn't know whether John had seen my car parked in his street or whether the nosy woman next door might have told him that someone had come looking for them.

At the Square, while Mac looked after the kids in the car, Jenny rushed into Kmart with some cash I'd given her for clothes while I cruised Woolworths with a trolley, flinging food and other basic stores into it. My last stop was the cash machine for funds to tide Jenny over. Then we drove straight to Wolf's house.

First, I went in through the small gate using one of the keys Wolf had given me which I always kept on my keyring when Wolf was away. I then went straight away to pick up the remote control from the hall table, and opened the driveway gate. Mac drove the car in and I shut the gates.

Wolf's high fence and the fact that his home was on a hilly corner block meant that people could not see in unless they sat on the fence or looked down from a tall tree. None of the houses on either side was more than one story high.

We settled everyone into the house, stocking the refrigerator with food, and enjoying all the comforts available in Wolf's up-market home because he always left the electricity and water turned on while he was away.

Wolf's house was a four-bedroom modern brick place. There was a downstairs lounge room across the width of the house and up six steps was a kitchen dining room and TV room which led out onto a courtyard at the back.

Up another flight of stairs were the bedrooms with a large deck off the main bedroom, overlooking a side garden. It was roomy and well-appointed with an eclectic mix of furniture, paintings, and knickknacks, most of them from Germany.

While the children explored the lounge, kitchen and TV room, at last I could talk at length with Jenny to find out more about John's state of mind, her physical and emotional suffering and whether the children had noticed his strange behaviour, as well as what our plan of action should be.

'Jenny, we'll only phone you when we're at a friend's house – in case John tries to track our calls somehow. We also won't drive around to see you for a while. We can't take any chances in case John follows us here. But we'll keep in phone contact until this is sorted. You're not frightened here, are you? John has no idea this place even exists. I know you're wary of contacting the police and I understand that. Let's give it a couple of days and see if he calms down and comes to his senses – or whether it's more serious than that. You need time to clear your head and work out whether there's anything more we can do now, as well as what you want to do in the long-term.'

I slipped her my credit card to use whenever she needed, and gave her the pin number. 'This'll tide you over. You'll be able to buy food online and have it delivered.'

Jenny nodded, tears welling in her eyes, and she hugged me tight. I felt we'd done everything we could for the time being.

'We have to go,' I whispered. 'We'd better get home in case John calls.'

Within an hour of arriving home, the phone rang. I took a big breath and picked it up.

'Hello.'

John's angry voice lashed down the phone line. 'Where is she? What have you done with her?'

'John, is that you?' I said lightly, trying to sound as if I was amazed to hear his voice. 'What do you mean? Has Jenny contacted you? Have you found her? Where has she been? Is she all right?'

'You know very well where she is. And I'm here to get her.'

'John, we haven't seen her. Where are you?'

'I've just arrived at your house. Open the door.'

At that moment we heard a banging on the door. Mac went to open it and was knocked aside by John pushing his way into the lounge room. He stamped into all the downstairs rooms, slamming the kitchen door back against the wall and rattling every cupboard in the room. He then ran upstairs and we heard him flinging each of the three bedroom doors open as well as the wardrobe doors. He moved on to the bathroom and the study, shouldering the doors open, looking in the shower and the sliding storage in the study. Mac and I just stood in the lounge room not saying a word. We had never seen him like this.

As he swept into the lounge room, again he turned to face us.

His cheeks were red, his mouth twisted into an angry scowl. He was spitting words out at us. With his fist almost in Mac's face, he growled, 'I'll find her. I know she must be staying here somewhere, and I'll get her – and you.'

He strode past Mac and out the door. Mac and I collapsed on the lounge chairs. I was shaking with fear. This man was a person we had not known at all. He seemed more than ready to harm us if he needed to.

'Mac, what a horrible man! I'm so glad Jenny is safely away from him. How lucky we were to have Wolf's place for Jenny to hide, so that brute can't find any sign of her here. I can't think what to do next, can you?'

Mac was still stunned. 'He seemed so violent. I've never seen him like that before. I guess he was angry because he thinks he's been found out lying to us about Jenny leaving him and also because he thinks we've taken her. Still, he's hurt our Jenny and is even prepared to flee with the children. He's a danger to them all. I wonder what has made him change?'

'Mac, I think we need to work out a plan to get through all this, because I think Jenny is kind of immobilised from fear. We've actually helped Jenny and the kids to leave him but what next? Although he's not sure we've done this, I think he'll pursue us until he is sure.'

I ticked off my ideas on my fingers. 'We could phone the police.'

'I'm not sure about that, Lilli. They would need to know the whole story. And we'd need to include Jenny in any report to the police. Let's ask her what she wants to do first. Let's give her a bit of time. It's a huge shock.'

I was still thinking about what we should do.

'We must never talk about knowing where Jenny is. And I even think we must never visit Wolf's house. John might find out. It would be so easy for him to follow us.'

I sat up suddenly. 'There's another thing I think we need to do and that is to put funds onto the credit card so that she won't be short of money for food.'

I started to get up but Mac held me back.

'Of course. Good idea. It can wait a few minutes though … or a few hours. Just take it easy for a bit or you'll be the one with high blood pressure next,' Mac said, easing back down.

We sat slumped back in our lounge chairs for some time, each of us thinking about what had happened.

'At least we've got Jenny and the kids back. I feel better now that we have her safe.'

'Yes, so do I. But I don't think this is the end of it, by any means. I think it's just the beginning,' he added.

Over the next few days we went about our regular tasks of shopping, gardening, hobbies and visits to the doctor for Mac. Every now and then I would think of Jenny and the children and I would smile to myself, even though there was a sense of fear lurking in the background of my thoughts. I phoned Jenny three times a day from friends' places. Even so, Jenny was getting a bit stir crazy, hidden away from the world and the children kept in and away from childcare and kindy.

On Wednesday, I drove to my regular art class laden down with essential tools and a canvas book of art paper. I'd been working on a watercolour of ivy leaves on a brick wall in muted autumn tones, and wanted to keep to my usual routine in case John was keeping a watch on us. Keeping busy was also a distraction from constantly worrying about the situation.

I first noticed a blue Mazda 2 nearby when I parked in the community hall carpark and then again when I came out from art class. I thought nothing of it at first. Just another senior going to a hobby class, to my mind.

But when the Mazda was still a few cars behind me as I neared home, I began to think I was being followed. Was this just paranoia because of our problem or was it real? Surely if I was being followed by John he would keep himself hidden better than that, I thought. Or maybe he wanted us to know he was following us to make us scared.

I decided this was my imagination at work and drove into our carport, slammed the car door, clicked it locked and went inside.

'How was art, Lilli?' Mac's voice called from the kitchen.

We sat at the kitchen table and I told him about my latest minor achievements at art class.

'By the way, I thought I was being followed today,' I said, and went on to describe what had happened.

'Hmm. Well, it's not a bad idea to keep a look out for something like that. I imagine that's what I'd do if I was John and believed we had Jenny with us.'

The next day we went shopping together. Both Mac and I kept scanning the road and cars near us in the carpark until we happened to see each other simultaneously and burst into laughter. We must have looked like very bad spies in a comedy movie.

It was the first time we had genuinely laughed in days and it felt good.

It wasn't long before the fear came back though, because as we turned into our street, we spied a blue Mazda several doors up. There was a man sitting in the car. Was it John?

Mac drove towards the car and I prepared to jump out and accost him, when the man started up the car and drove off in the other direction. Although we strained our eyes to see the driver we couldn't make him out.

At least we weren't paranoid. We were being followed.

Chapter 7

Mac and I had decided at the very beginning that we would not talk about Jenny or the children, even to friends. The possibility of being overheard by neighbours or friends seemed even more real now that we knew we were being followed.

So we put away the shopping and went for a walk.

'I think we shouldn't even acknowledge that we've noticed the car following us,' I said.

'A bit late now, Lilli, after getting so close to it,' Mac said. 'But I do think we need to be very cautious.'

'If I was John and was following us,' I ruminated, 'I might think it strange that we're not more upset than we seem to be, and strange that we're not alerting our friends – or even the police. If he's watching us or even creeping around the outside of our place at night, he must be surprised at our silence and inaction, that we're not talking to people about her.'

'You're right. I think we need to talk about Jenny and the children as if they're still missing.'

'Should we go to the police and tell them John has threatened us?'

'I don't know,' Mac said. 'I think John would just say he was angry because his wife has left him and that would be that. They wouldn't charge him with anything so what would be the point?'

At times I was very tearful and angry, concerned that John would come back and abuse us or even hurt us. We'd been able to phone Jenny a few times on our pre-paid phone when we were out on a walk or at a friend's home. Now she was adamantly declaring that she didn't want us to go to the police, as that would mean she'd have to tell them the whole story.

'I don't want him to know where we are yet,' she insisted. 'I need time for all this to settle down, for John to get back to something like normal.'

She was tearful each time we spoke, but was holding up. The children had asked where their daddy was and she had told them that he'd had to go overseas for his work. This sounded quite rational to Chiara, as he'd been on jobs in the USA and England before.

The garden at Wolf's house was quite big, so the children were having fun exploring it. The only people who came to the door were the delivery people for online meat, dairy and vegetables, and a Mormon couple who came to the gate one afternoon.

We told Jenny we loved her and to keep on guard.

After about a fortnight I decided to take stock of our finances. I sat at the computer and looked at the figures. We had a house free of debt and two cars, but cash was tight. We were now supporting two families and purchasing a lot of extra items – all because of John. Maybe we would have to sell one of the cars before long, or if the worst possible thing happened and money became an issue, we might even be pushed to sell our house and move somewhere smaller. All very complicated. Just a standby plan, I thought, as I felt some responsibility as the mainstay of the family now, with Jenny a kind of captive as a result of John's threatening behaviour.

I visited Tony and Samantha a few times and told them bits of the story. We had not told them about Mac going to hospital with high blood pressure but we were definitely not going to tell them about finding and hiding Jenny and the kids. We felt that it might put Tony and Samantha in jeopardy.

Tony was very angry and threatened to go find John and give him 'what for'. I persuaded him not to, as this would only cause more conflict.

He thought for a moment or two.

'Mum, I think we've been followed too. I've noticed a blue Mazda 2 down the street that's there at different hours of the day and night. It certainly doesn't belong to anyone in our small street. In fact it might be here now.'

We carefully pulled back the curtains at the large front windows a little and I could see a blue Mazda 2 with someone sitting inside several doors down the street.

Tony rushed downstairs before I could stop him and jogged up to the car. We watched from the window as the car started and roared swiftly away, making black skid marks on the tarmac, and just missing Tony by a whisker.

Tony had jumped back, falling backwards on to the grass verge. He was furious when he got back in the house, brushing dirt from his trousers as he entered.

'This is too much,' he said.

'Yes,' I said, 'it is. The problem for us is that we don't have any proof that it's John who is stalking us.'

I said my goodbyes to Tony and set off for home. I felt as if we were being controlled by unknown forces and our happy life had become fearful and strange Perhaps that was how Jenny had been feeling for a long time now, so I shouldn't complain, I thought. After all, we had her and the children back close to us and out of harm's way.

It was time to think about what to do next. Wolf would be back from Germany in four months so that should be time enough to have dealt with John and have Jenny and the kids back on track.

We thought we should have one more try at speaking to John. We needed to convince him that we didn't have Jenny or the children with us, and he should accept the fact that he and Jenny had separated, and think about what was best for the children. Then he might stop following us – because we were sure that it was him in the blue Mazda. But when we'd tried to speak to him before, we found he'd changed his mobile number, so now we didn't have any way to contact him.

It occurred to us to phone John's parents, Betty and Sid, in England. They might have been in contact and would have his new number.

We didn't know them at all, as they hadn't come to the wedding in Australia. But I did have an address for them because we'd sent them an invitation, even though they hadn't replied.

We went online to find their phone number from the address and name we had. It took a while but eventually we found the right number and, as England was 10 hours behind Australia, we stayed up late to phone to make sure we had a time when they would be home.

'Hello.' A woman's voice with an English accent, of course. 'Who's this?'

'We're John's parents-in-law,' I said. 'Is that Betty?'

'Oh,' came the reply, 'Lisa's parents, Mr and Mrs Turnbull?'

'Who?' I asked.

'I'm sorry. Lisa has nothing to do with us now that she's come out of hospital. I suppose she's still in London if you are looking for her,' she continued as if I hadn't said a thing.

I had no idea what she was talking about or indeed who Mr and Mrs Turnbull and Lisa were. All I could think was how difficult communication could be when speaking to someone from a different country and with a different accent. So I started again, slowly this time.

I explained who I was, that we had lost John's number and wanted to contact him. The reason sounded very dodgy to me, as why would we want his number when we could just speak to his wife, our daughter?

But she didn't even question this, instead explaining that Lisa was John's long-time girlfriend who he'd abused and injured, and launching into a tirade that shocked me.

'We don't see John. He's been trouble ever since he was a child. We never want to see him again.'

'Oh dear,' I said. 'What happened?'

'Right from the start he seemed very needy and wanted us to pay attention only to him. We thought that if we showed him lots of attention and love, he would grow out of this as most children do. Just like all parents though, we disciplined him when he was naughty. And every time, he would find a way to get his revenge.'

'How did he do that?' I asked, already feeling apprehensive about the answer to come.

Betty had obviously stored up a lot of anger about John and was ready to let it all out.

'When he was seven years old we took away his bike for a week because he'd been out on the streets late at night after tea. The next week all our tyres were let down on both cars. Another time we sent him to his room for being rude and he cut up all the sheets on our bed. As he grew older we thought he had grown out of this revengeful attitude. But no, he got worse. We tried psychologists, but had no success. The last thing he did, when we wouldn't give him any money to buy a car, was to set fire to the house while my husband was asleep. It was lucky I came home in time to wake him. We've never seen him since then and good riddance to him.'

'Oh … Thank you for telling me this. I don't know what to say to you,' I said. 'Do you remember that our daughter married him? We sent you an invitation to the wedding.'

'I didn't know that,' Betty said. 'When we get any correspondence from Australia we throw it away, as John is the only person we know who lives there. I feel sorry for your daughter. And you, just watch yourselves. He can't be trusted if he's crossed.'

I related the conversation to Mac. He was very angry.

'Oh, Lilli, I wish we'd spoken to the parents before Jenny married him. I wish we'd seen some clues to his behaviour. I'm worried now that because he thinks we took Jenny away, he'll continue to follow us and harass us and, now we know that, he could even take his revenge out on us.'

'It's worrying – because we did take Jenny. Although now, under the circumstances, I'm sure that what we did was for the best.'

'Yes, this knowledge about his vengeful character puts a different light on the situation. I certainly don't want him to find Jenny and take revenge on her. I think we should just go about our regular business. If he wants to follow me to the doctor and bowls, and you to art, creative writing and ukulele classes, so be it.'

We were both silent as we thought about Jenny.

What has she got herself into? What can I do with a man who takes his revenge every time there's conflict? Okay, no police just yet, until I get a better handle on how this man, someone I used to trust as my son-in-law, might act.

It was now a cat and mouse game until John showed his hand. Above all, I thought, Jenny, Chiara and Ryan would have to stay in hiding, and we would have to stay alert to any harm that John might have in store for us.

Chapter 8

We tried to stick to routine things. Mac went to bowls on Monday morning. I went to art on Wednesday and a séance party on Thursday afternoon across the road at our neighbour, Jean's place.

I really didn't want to go, but knew that if I stayed home I would only worry about Jenny and the children and get angrier at John.

I had been to a séance before when Jenny and Tony were little. It too had been an Ouija board party and, because the friend who had arranged it was a believer of ghosts and such, she had organised a scribe to take down all the conversations and contacts with the spirits. Being a bit of a cynic, I found myself grinning when she had called out in a sing-song voice, 'Any spirits there?'

It had been fascinating to see the upside down shot-glass we were using, spin across the board and spell out words. I had taken my fingers off the board occasionally, and also at other times, pushed the glass to see what would happen. My own little science experiments, I suppose. In the end I'd given up and just gone along with the energy of the group.

Back then, the scribe had noted that an Aunt Rika from Holland was the spirit the board had summoned. She'd killed herself in an attic when she was not allowed to marry the man of her choice. All this drama was found out as questions were posed to the board.

It didn't help my cynical attitude much when my mother who was alive then, later told me that she had an Aunt Rika from Holland who'd done just that. When I'd told the friend about this coincidence, she said I must have been the medium between us and Aunt Rika. I became a big celebrity with the group for a while but refused politely to go to any more séances.

Now, thirty years on, I was going to another séance, just to keep my mind off our problems. I dressed in casual autumn-toned layered clothes – sensible and not too outlandish for such an occasion – and made up a plate of dip and biscuits.

I smiled to myself as I always did when I made a dish to take to a party. There had been a time early in our marriage when Mac had burst in the door saying we had been invited to a barbecue and we had to bring plates. I thought this was a bit strange, but dutifully got out two of our wedding plates and put them in a bag. It wasn't until we arrived and everyone was handing over plates of salad, cold meats and cakes that we realised that Mac had misheard plates for 'a plate', and I had naively thought that the hosts didn't have enough plates for guests.

We hardly ate a thing that day, we felt so embarrassed about eating other people's food.

Here I was all these years later, toddling off to my neighbour's house with a smile on my face. There were three others from various houses in the street and as we all knew each other well, we chatted away happily for a time before the séance began.

Margaret lived next door to me on the left and Sylvie lived three doors down from Margaret. Jean's house was directly opposite ours and Jackie was next door to her.

We had all lived in the street for thirty-odd years. Our children had grown up together and had all been in and out of our houses playing sport, practising ballet moves, listening and playing music and having sleepovers. All our children were now adults and we liked to swap photos of them, plus news of their love lives and our grandchildren, always groaning about how much babysitting we were asked to do while secretly loving every minute of it.

At first Mac and I had been determined we wouldn't talk to anyone about Jenny. And we'd stuck to it. But then we reasoned that if we hadn't rescued her and secreted her away, we would have been so upset we'd be talking to all our friends and asking them what they would do if they were in our place.

I waited for a break in the conversation to mention what had happened. Everyone was so sympathetic, caring and worried, gathering around to comfort me. I burst into tears and told them the story of trying to find her. I didn't say we had.

Jean from across the road suggested I ask the spirits. So we began to 'make contact' using another upside down shot-glass on a wooden board. After lots of interesting questions and answers from the board, I was pressured into asking if the spirit knew where my daughter was.

We waited for a few seconds, and although the glass had been travelling back and forward across the board before my question, it was now ominously still.

The séance packed up after that. Everyone was very disappointed. I guess they were hoping to get an address that I would be able to go to and be happily reunited with my daughter, all due to a spirit. I felt a bit guilty as I already knew where she was.

Then Jean spoke up.

'I wondered why that policeman came to my door the other day asking if I had seen anyone near your house other than you or Mac.'

'What?' I squawked. 'When was that?'

'Well, afternoon I noticed that policeman going into your house and then he came over to mine.'

I thought back to Monday afternoon. We'd gone for a walk. So there'd been no one home.

'How did you know he was a policeman? Was he in uniform?' I asked.

'He had a badge and announced he was from Dee Why police station, even though he was in plain clothes.'

'Yes,' Margaret piped up. 'He came to our house too. He must be helping to find your daughter.'

I gave my thanks for the interesting afternoon and the comfort they had extended to me, grabbed my plate, now empty, and rushed across the road. I was chilled to the bone.

'Mac,' I yelled as I came in the door.

'Did you contact a spirit?' He was smiling as he came out of the kitchen with a cup of tea. 'Are you going to live a long life and be rich and famous?'

'No, Mac, something's happened. Jean and Margaret say they've had visits from the plain clothes police asking if they've seen anyone near our house. Jean said she saw him go into our house. It was when we weren't home.'

By now Mac was taking me very seriously.

'Mac, someone's been in our house. And I reckon it wasn't the police because we haven't told them anything about Jenny being missing.'

Now he looked shocked. 'I wonder if John told the police ... or hired a private detective to come round and see if Jenny and the children were here.'

'I bet that's it. A private detective! That would be the sort of thing he'd do. That man might have even planted bugs in the house so he could listen to our conversations.'

At that, Mac and I fell silent. We looked around the room as if expecting to be able to spot a bug straight away. Then both of us moved towards the back door and out into the garden where we could speak freely.

We felt violated. How could I sleep in our bed knowing someone could just get in when they wanted to?

'I'll go straight down to Bunnings and buy bolts and padlocks for all the exterior doors and I'll use nails to lock our sash windows,' Mac announced.

'I'm coming with you. I can't stay here on my own until it's safe.'

'Right,' said Mac. 'Let's go.'

Later, I felt much better. I had changed the linen on our bed even though common sense told me that no one had been in our bed. I'd cleaned the bathroom from top to bottom and the kitchen too. I threw away all the food in the main part of the refrigerator because I couldn't bear the idea that anyone might have touched any of it.

Mac put bolts on the inside of each door. He also drilled holes in the window frames and the window sills so that a nail could be slotted down through both to hold them tight.

We looked in likely spots for bugs. On TV they were always found in light bulb fixtures, phone connections, under coffee tables or behind mirrors or pictures. We found nothing.

We hardly spoke, and when we did we were aware that someone might be listening from a device that we couldn't find so our voices sounded very stilted.

We felt violated.

Chapter 9

The next week started fine, with blue sky and fluffy clouds which always made me feel bright and cheerful. We talked with Jenny a few times and I told her about ukulele classes and how I was improving.

'We're getting a performance group together with a repertoire of Beatles and rock 'n roll songs,' I said.

'That's wonderful, Mum. I wish I could come and see you play.'

'Never mind. I'm thinking the kids might like a ukulele each. The coloured ones are only $20.'

'They'd love that. They need a few new activities.'

We chatted some more about the kids and how she was getting along at Wolf's house, then said goodbye with an 'I love you.

....

But by the middle of the week, anxiety and stress were getting to me. I misplaced my reading glasses every time I put them down, and I couldn't find the keys to the car on several occasions when we were going shopping. I also left my purse in the car when I was at ukulele practice and was very lucky that no one saw it and broke into the car to steal it.

So I wasn't surprised when I discovered all the pegs for the clothes line were in the tub of water in which I had been soaking some socks. Why did I do that, I thought?

Am I getting Alzheimer's or has the trauma of the past month sent my mind out of whack? If Mac can have high blood pressure due to trauma, I guess I can lose my mind.

The next day I was searching on the back step for our sneakers so that we could set off for a walk, when I just happened to look up at the trees around the garden and noticed the sneakers hanging by their laces from the wattle tree. I certainly hadn't remembered doing such a silly thing.

On Thursday after a shopping trip, Mac and I came home to our back verandah windows broken. It looked like someone had tried to get into the house.

Could this be John in an angry state of mind taking revenge or could it just be the neighbourhood kids, we wondered. Surely John wouldn't do anything illegal? I thought about how he'd tried to burn down his father's house with his father in it. We decided it could have been John trying to get in, after all. We were so frightened that we phoned the police straight away.

Two uniformed police arrived several hours later. The one in charge was 193 centimetres tall, an imposing guy. He looked down on me from his great height and even on Mac who was no shorty. I imagined that every criminal would quake in his or her shoes if accosted by him. The other was a very athletic woman with her hair tied back in a severe pony tail. She smiled at us and asked to come in.

'Sgt Ronson and Constable Bailey, here at your request. What's happened?'

We explained how we'd come home to find the windows broken and showed them the spot. They asked a range of general questions, most of which we either couldn't answer or replied to with a 'No'. Questions such as, 'Did they enter the house?' 'Is anything missing?' and 'Do you have any enemies?'

Mac and I looked at each other for this last question. Could we tell them what we thought? Would they believe us? Almost as one telepathic thought, we both said no.

They suggested that it was probably kids as nothing had been stolen. They also said they couldn't do anything without some proof of who the intruders were. They gave us the name of a security firm who could place cameras and sensor lights in strategic places around the outside of the home. They also said they would put our address on the night patrol police car list for our street.

I asked how often this would occur and they answered that it would probably be once or twice a fortnight at a variety of times, day and evenings. Well, that's pretty useless, I thought.

We quietly cleaned up the rubbish and called the security firm. They came that afternoon.

On their advice we also purchased a key pad code for the front and back doors with an alarm that went straight to their company. Their policy stated that they would be there in 10-20 minutes if the alarm sounded.

I had confessed to Mac the other things that had been happening to me and how I thought I was going mad. Mac hugged me and told me how silly I was, as there was not a saner person that he knew anywhere.

Over the next few days though, we realised that the harassment and fear tactics would only become worse.

The first day after the security had been heightened, two tyres were let down on my car after I left it on the street during the afternoon. Unfortunately the cameras were not pointed at where I was parked on the street.

I rushed across to Jean and to the two neighbours on either side of us to ask if they'd seen anyone near our house but none of them were home. It occurred to me that as it was Friday and a regular weekly shopping day, whoever had done this had watched and waited until the neighbours had gone out before attacking the car.

Once again we called the police.

They didn't come around to our house this time but asked if the cameras had caught any movement. I explained that the cameras were trained on the house and side paths so there were no photos. They took a note of the situation and agreed to add more police patrols to our street as a deterrent.

Of course Mac and I thought that John was the culprit and this would never deter him. We wondered how he knew that we had new tight security and cameras which he was able to dodge.

On the third call to the police in three days, after a pile of black garbage bags filled with putrid rubbish was thrown on our front lawn, a new person came to see us.

He was probably in his forties, a well-built man in a smart suit, with a shine on his shoes. He introduced himself as Detective Rogers. He looked interested in our story and seemed to understand our fear.

For the first time Mac and I felt we could tell him our story. The only part we missed out was the part where we had rescued Jenny and the children. We had agreed that we would never tell this part for we understood how word could get around even if it was not meant to.

'Why do you think it's your son-in-law?' he asked.

'This harassment all started when Jenny, our daughter, left him. I think he believes we helped her to do so.' I blushed as I spoke this blatant half-truth.

'I can go and talk to him if you like. Check out the truth of the matter. Caution him if I get the feeling he's guilty.'

I sat up straight. 'Oh, no, I don't want that. It might not be him. After all, he is our son-in-law. And it might make it worse.' I was frantic to stop him from following up by talking to John.

Detective Rogers put his note book away in his pocket. He sighed, 'If you don't want this then the best thing to do is take photos of any strange cars you see parked on your road or that seem to be following you. Perhaps you'll find it's not your son-in-law but someone completely different,' he said.

We agreed to do this and after he left, Mac set about finding our camera. Both of us wished we hadn't spoken to Detective Rogers about the possibility of the person being John.

All this anxiety had distracted our minds from the main issue of finding somewhere for Jenny and the children to go when Wolf returned. Mac had an idea which was a sound one.

'We could get a new identity for Jenny and the children and then find another part of Australia where she could live. Somewhere away from Sydney – like Hobart or Perth.'

We discussed the idea at some length, imagining how they could start again in a new place with no fear of being found. We knew that Chiara would begin school in February and would need to show her birth certificate. We even thought about how we could visit them all on holiday, and if we were clever, John wouldn't know we were visiting them. At last, reality stopped this wishful thinking with my question.

'How do we get her a new identity?'

We didn't have a clue about how to go about it.

Mac looked on the internet but it looked complicated and lengthy to legally change your name, and there was certainly no way anyone could stand in for another person in making an application. Jenny was too frightened to even go out at this stage.

We thought about all the people we knew. They all seemed too suburban and nice to know such things.

On Wednesday afternoon I went to my creative writing class. There were about ten of us who met every second week to discuss and critique our work.

I thought I might ask them how they would go about getting a new identity. I could pretend that it was for a story I was going to write. Paul, a tall bearded fellow who'd been a film director might know something, I thought, because he could have met some shady characters on his travels around the world. There was also Neil, who always researched his subjects thoroughly and in such detail that I thought he might be able to find out some information for us.

When asked, both Paul and Neil said they would give it some

consideration and let me know at the next meeting.

Later, Pam, the leader of the writing group, talked about creating opportunities in a story to kill off some characters, especially those you as an author weren't fond of, and I had a thought: *John would give up harassing us if there were no Jenny or children.*

The idea caught hold of my mind so that I couldn't wait to finish our session and get home to Mac.

I had to sit through a whole session hearing everyone's writing efforts for that week. Keith had written about a time during his childhood when a plane had crashed into a mountain range near his home town. Sissy had written about adventures in America, Charlotte had a story about the highs and lows of travelling in Canada, and Sean was composing a period story about Lasseter and his search for a reef of gold.

The writers all had different writing styles and interests and they chatted back and forth about their work. All the group's members seemed interested in finding out about changing a person's identity. I imagined they would put the ideas into future scripts themselves.

I commented where needed and gave positive feedback about the turn of phrase or any colourful words or interesting ideas that I noticed in a story. They were all experienced writers and always caused me to marvel at their skill and creativity. But this time my mind was not quite with them.

At home, I waited for Mac to come back from the doctor. His blood pressure results had been quite encouraging over the previous three weeks despite the harassment we'd been experiencing.

This time though I didn't even wait until he had taken off his coat, to grab his arm and drag him out into the back garden to tell him about my idea.

'Let's kill off Jenny and the children, or rather, let's pretend we've killed off Jenny and the children,' I said. Or something to that effect.

Chapter 10

Jenny sat on the back steps of Wolf's house watching the children play.

She had just washed her blonde curly hair and dyed it brown and then put on her jeans and a cream top. She brushed strands of hair away from her eyes and tucked them behind her ears.

For once she looked and felt great.

Each night she had hardly been able to sleep. Her stomach had been in knots and her thoughts had spiralled round and round trying to solve the problem of what to do and where to go next.

While her parents had kept the funds coming in and had stated that Wolf would not need his house for a few more weeks, Jenny knew she couldn't leave it until the last minute to find a solution. She needed to get out of Sydney. She needed to hide from John. She felt that she couldn't do it alone.

She was torn between thoughts of what John might do if he found her, and what she could do with limited finances and options for work.

With a degree in Education, Jenny had once been a kindergarten teacher, before starting her swim school. But how could she use that experience to get a job now? She was sure that teaching would be the first place John would look. There was probably a register of teachers across the State, probably even across the whole of Australia.

She began to shake uncontrollably and sob quietly and then forced herself to stop. The children needed her calm and caring, not anxious and sad.

She glanced at them playing happily in the mud at the base of the dripping outdoor tap. They were having fun. How did I get here, she thought? I wonder how long this will last. Which led her to reminisce ...

She'd met John when she was at university studying Visual Arts. He'd been in the rugby football club's final game after attending a short course on IT, while she'd been sitting relaxing and enjoying the game between lectures. At the end of the game, a young man came running up the stairs to her stand and sat beside her.

'I noticed you sitting here. What did you think of the game, and my try?'

'Oh dear, I didn't see it,' Jenny said.

'Well, that's all right because I missed it. I just wanted to see if you were watching or gazing into space.'

'I'm afraid I was just daydreaming.'

'My name's John. John Stanford.' He held out his hand and Jenny shook it. His hand was warm, large and encompassed her small fingers. She noticed he had short neat fingernails.

Jenny looked up from his hand into the bluest eyes she had ever seen. It was as if they were laughing down at her.

'The game's finished. Come for a coffee at the cafeteria?'

'Okay,' Jenny said, making an instant decision that the next class was only a review of part of the semester's work and could be missed.

If only things had stayed like that day. It had been full of laughter and discussion on topics that either she was interested in or had a comment about. When they left the cafeteria at 8 o'clock that evening John had already asked her for a date.

Was it my fault that things changed, she asked herself? She thought back through the ten years of marriage. She knew a change in John had started when Chiara was born five years before.

It always seemed that John became very jealous when my attention was on her. That's when he started checking up on me, reading the odometer to see how many miles I'd driven that day, to match it against where I'd said I'd been. That's when he started doling out the week's money and asking for receipts for everything. If it didn't tally, he was cross and I had to explain where the money had gone.

There was one time when I couldn't account for $10 and that's when he hit me for the first time. He was so ashamed and so contrite, that I forgave him. Every time he hit me he was sorry and I forgave him. Even when I began to see the pattern of anger, then contrition, I was too embarrassed to tell anyone. Now I can see that I've just let my life slide by, doing nothing about it.

I haven't loved John for a long time. I think I've forgotten about me for the sake of the children. John has taken away my confidence and made me feel as if I'm not capable of looking after myself without him there to direct me.

Jenny wiped tears from her cheeks. *Once I was a confident, happy girl with a wonderful life ahead of me. Now …*

She didn't finish the thought. The children rushed up to her.

'Come and see our shop, Mummy. It's got leaves and flowers and mud pies in it.'

Jenny bought some pies at the pretend shop and went back to her seat on the step. She was restless and alone. She'd been at home without speaking to another adult except her parents for three weeks. She thought she would start to go mad.

She knew her mum and dad were trying to find a solution for her predicament. They were thinking about how to find a new identity for her, but she thought this was an impossible idea. If only she could get out and find a solution for herself. Yet it was clear that she couldn't leave her kids, she couldn't expose herself to places where John might look for her and she didn't know how to start to find a long-term solution, anyway.

The house next door had been up for rent for two weeks, but she now heard sounds coming from the garden. A man leant over the six foot wall from next door and startled her.

'Hello,' he said. 'I've just rented this house for a month while I'm here in Sydney on business. Just thought I'd say hello and invite you over for morning tea.'

Jenny jumped at the voice, twisting around with a scared look on her face. She tried to hide it by looking everywhere but at him.

'Sorry I startled you. It's all right, I understand if you don't want to, although I'm just a country guy who's alone in a big city.'

Jenny looked up and saw a really nice genuine smile on a clear-eyed, honest looking and rather handsome face. He was dressed in a checked shirt with a wide leather belt, and the rest of him was hidden by the wall.

'You can't be that tall, you must be standing on a ladder,' she laughed.

'Yeah, I found the ladder in the shed and I could hear you and the children laughing and playing. My sister's kids sound just like that when they're having fun, so I was a bit homesick.'

'Why don't you come over here?' Jenny asked. 'I can't leave the kids alone.'

'Right,' he said and disappeared from view. The next moment, she heard a knock on the gate door which she always kept locked.

They spent the afternoon chatting about general things like the TV programs they liked and the sport they followed. Jenny wasn't a great fan of rugby league or rugby but she took an interest in soccer, and vaguely supported the Matildas, whereas Jed Willis seemed to have a worldwide knowledge of football. He often woke in the night to catch a game televised from the other side of the world.

Every now and then Jenny got up to deal with a fight between the children or to get them drinks and snacks. Jed seemed very nice and she couldn't help comparing him to John. Jed explained that he'd come to Sydney for a business meeting to do with his cattle property in Victoria. He had an arrangement in place to provide meat for a group of restaurants and he was here to discuss their needs.

'Why have you chosen a house in the suburbs instead of a hotel in the city?' Jenny asked him, adding, 'Not that it's any of my business.'

Jed laughed, his eyes crinkling up in a pleasant manner. 'I hate that falseness of hotels and motels and the loneliness of them. I googled Sydney and this property came up. It seemed just what I needed. My mum died a few years back and I'm not married, so I don't have to have a grand place. This just suited my lifestyle.'

'What sort of cattle do you have?' Jenny inquired.

'Vealers. I guess you might not know about them. They're young cattle and the meat that comes from them is called veal.'

'Oh,' said Jenny, 'I wondered why it was called veal. Veal Parmigiana or crumbed veal. Yummy.'

Jed chuckled at that, and Jenny thought how relaxed his laugh sounded and how genuine he seemed.

'Best I get back to work. I've got to prepare for a meeting this afternoon. Perhaps I can drop in tomorrow?'

'I'd like that,' Jenny said. 'Give me a call so I can have the gate open.'

As he disappeared around the corner of the block, Jenny considered she'd never had such an enjoyable morning, and felt she'd made a friend.

While the issues with John had still been in the back of her mind, she had been able to forget them for a few moments at a time, and just enjoy talking to another adult. An adult who had no ulterior motive. He hadn't wanted her to admire him as a fine specimen of a man. He hadn't wanted to make a date. He had just enjoyed finding out what she was thinking and wanted to discuss the world in general.

She couldn't help comparing him to John, even though this seemed terribly disloyal. Silly really, considering she was in hiding from John. John, who was always trying to trip her up, as if he wanted to discover that she'd been out with another man. It occurred to her that he wanted to prove that he was right about her and that she was not a faithful wife.

Over time she had learnt to be careful about what she said so there could be no misunderstandings that would lead to a fit of jealousy, even with the local corner shop owner who was at least seventy years old. She realised now that she hadn't had a carefree conversation with another man for some years. Even talks with her parents had always been vetted in her mind before she spoke, as she had always been wary of saying something that might alert them to John's behaviour.

A new feeling of confidence washed over her and she was able to call the children in to lunch in a much happier mood. Even the children noticed and Ryan said, 'Mummy, you are very happy today,' as he munched on his sandwich.

Jenny couldn't deny it.

Chapter 11

'What man? What's going on?' I squeaked into the phone as Mac and I strolled down to the beach for one of our walks.

I turned to Mac, horrified.

'A man next door?' I asked. 'Someone you've just met. You've known him for a week and you think he's great.'

Mac looked worried. I turned up the volume of the phone so that Mac could hear what Jenny was saying too.

'It's all right, Mum. He's very nice. A country guy, from Victoria. He's already a true friend.'

'But Jenny …' Mac bellowed into the phone, clutching my wrist in a tight grip, '… he might be a private detective or a friend of John's who's discovered where you are and is checking out the scene, in order to take you and the children away from us again.'

I could hear the anxiety in Mac's voice as he said this. Jenny could hear it too.

'Don't worry, Dad. He's shown me pictures of his property on his phone and he has nothing to do with John. In fact, he didn't even know my name when he first met me.'

Mac and I glanced at each other nervously.

'Jenny, I'm coming around straight away,' I said.

As Mac and I hurried home, puffing our way along, I outlined a plan.

'Just in case John is watching us, let's foil him. I'll go across the road and ask Jean if she will take me to Wolf's house and I'll make an excuse that my car battery is flat. At the same time you drive off in the other car. I'll say you have a doctor's appointment and can't take me. That way John would have to choose who to follow. It won't be me because he would think that I wouldn't go to Jenny with a neighbour in tow. I'll ring you to pick me up later from a bus stop.'

I looked up and down the road but couldn't see a blue Mazda. But that didn't mean that John hadn't changed cars or wasn't waiting around the corner.

Mac fiddled about in his car until I had convinced Jean to take me in her car. It didn't take long as she was happy to help.

We set off. I got out several doors down from Wolf's house just in case I was being followed and also so that Jean wouldn't know which house I was going into. I waved until the car had disappeared and then I walked along past Wolf's house and up the road for about five minutes until I was as sure as I could be that I wasn't being followed. Then I turned back to Jenny.

She met me at the gate.

'Jed is here. I thought I would ask him round to meet you as you seemed so stressed about it. Don't look so cross or worried. He's just a nice guy.'

Yeah, murderers and kidnappers always look like nice guys.

I think Jed could see that I wasn't happy about him being there. He must have decided I was quite mad to be quizzing him as if our daughter was still fifteen, not thirty. But he took it all in good humour and answered my questions calmly. It was Jenny who was quite put out by my questions.

'Mum,' she whined on a number of occasions when I asked a rather pointed question of Jed.

But I couldn't stop. This was my daughter and her children I was protecting. Mac and I had gone to such lengths to help her and we couldn't have it all fall through because of one false step.

I noticed how the kids came up to Jed and spoke to him happily and how he responded to them in an easy-going way. I also noticed how he laughed and chatted with Jenny and how often they touched each other in passing – when I wasn't asking him some awfully private question that I had no right to ask. I wondered if they were falling in love?

Little by little I became less concerned about him. Still, even though a little part of me wanted to respond positively to him, another part of me kept saying that this could be a trap. And uncertainties kept flying into my thoughts.

How can you tell if someone is going to hurt you? Do you have to know them for a long while or is one day or one week enough? Can I trust my sense of right and wrong? How many people have been taken in by confidence tricksters or murderers? There are hundreds of men in prison who seemed nice to start with.

My conclusion was that maybe we had to trust Jenny's judgement of character in this matter even though Jenny had already made one mistake with John.

What could Mac and I do about it? Jenny was happier than I had seen her for a long time. She had to spend a few more weeks at Wolf's house alone and here was someone to talk to. He didn't seem to be harmful as far as I could tell. Was I a good judge of character? I didn't know anymore. I was startled when Jenny bumped my shoulder.

'Mum.'

I hadn't realised that I'd been staring at Jed for the longest time. Jenny was embarrassed and so it seemed was Jed, who was busy brushing down his trousers after he'd sat on the grass. He was looking anywhere but at me.

I decided to have a final word with Jenny as she took me to the gate.

'Sorry …,' I said. 'Just thinking ...'

I took a breath before going on.

'Jenny dear, he seems nice but you know how worried your dad and I are about you. We think that John could be up to all sorts of nasty tricks. I told her about the phone calls we had made to his parents in London and about the things that were happening at our house. I hadn't planned on telling her all this but thought that she needed to be on her guard and the only way to convince her of this was to tell her everything that had happened.

Jenny began to cry. 'Oh, Mum, I didn't know this would happen to you. It's not right. You need to leave me to figure this out for myself.' She hugged me and I hugged her back.

'We're here to help and get you settled away from John. We'll figure this out together. Besides you can't do it alone with two kids. I just wanted to tell you so that you would know why we were worried about

Jed. We want to you to be on your guard at all times.'

'I will be, Mum,' Jenny said, as she gave me a last hug and showed me out the gate. I hoped she was right.

I walked for quite a while until I was nowhere near Wolf's house and then phoned Mac to come and pick me up.

The idea of pretending to kill Jenny and the kids came back into my mind as I walked. Mac stared at me when I mentioned it again.

'Are you mad?'

'I don't think so,' I faltered.

'Come on, Lilli, what would you do? How could you produce bodies to prove they were dead? Would there be an inquest? After all, three dead people would raise an alarm. The police would immediately begin a thorough investigation.'

He laughed.

'Are you going round the bend?'

I began to think logically about this and realised that it was just wishful thinking on my part and was really a completely mad idea.

'Sorry,' I said meekly. 'I guess it was a slightly screwy idea. I'm just at my wits' end to know what to do. Especially as Jenny has to leave Wolf's house in about two to three weeks.'

I looked out the window to see if I could spot a blue Mazda as we approached our house. Then I gasped in shock.

There was a tip truck backed up to the front lawn. A worker in shorts, a singlet and working boots was using a shovel to help the soil slide down the tail gate to an enormous pile on the front path and lawn.

Mac braked in the drive and hurried down to the fellow.

'Hi, mate,' he said. 'What's going on?'

'Just delivering your soil. I was told you wouldn't mind if we dumped it on the lawn even though you were out. Top soiling your garden, are you?'

Mac said, 'We didn't order any soil.'

'Got the delivery docket and receipt right here, mate.' The fellow leaned in and grabbed the paperwork from the dashboard of his truck.

Mac looked at it. It was certainly correct. The soil had been ordered and paid for and the address was correct.

We didn't know what to do. We couldn't ask this workman to shovel it all back into the truck and take it away. It was not his fault. We didn't want the soil, especially if it had any connection with John. We knew that this was a new form of harassment from John. We waved the truck off and gazed at the pile.

'Perhaps we could suggest that all our neighbours come and take a barrow full for their gardens,' I said. 'If John is somewhere watching, he will be angry that we are not annoyed at the soil delivery, as I think he meant us to be, and that we have solved the problem of a pile of soil on our lawn.'

'That's a great idea,' Mac said. 'Although I guess if he's watching somewhere it will just make him madder still.'

Chapter 12

Mac and I tried to remain calm even though a wave of events kept happening to us. Every week there was something new.

On Monday I discovered the sheets had been dragged down off the line and torn into pieces. The sheets happened to be new and I was angry.

The following week the back window of the laundry was smashed and glass fell into the laundry tubs inside. I hadn't noticed this until I was washing something by hand in the tub of warm water and saw blood on my hands. I had cut myself on the shards of glass.

Mac and I began to examine everything every time we came in from a walk or outing. Once the back door screen was slashed, another time the plants around the steps were pulled out of the ground and strewn across the garden.

We had never seen John and neither had our next door neighbours when I asked them if they had seen anyone in our garden.

Each time something happened, we had to hire tradespeople to fix it or buy new materials or even spend a day cleaning up the mess ourselves.

I got angrier and angrier as things seemed to escalate.

Our neighbour suggested we get camera lights in the back garden as that seemed to be where all the destruction was occurring.

We called the security company again and workers positioned extra sensor lights and cameras trained onto the garden. The night after this, the lights turned on at 7pm and again at 1am, set off by someone moving about. Mac and I rushed out into the garden each time, Mac with a club in his hand that we had brought back from a holiday in Fiji. We scanned the garden but saw nothing. After the second warning lights were set off in the middle of the night, we turned on the camera, hoping to see John sneaking around so we could tell the police.

All we saw was a ringtail possum. It crossed the lawn at 7pm, and recrossed it back to the big tree next door at 1am. This was obviously his nightly trail. I recalled that possums were known to take the same routes to a patch where they would find food, at the same time each night. Mac and I laughed when we saw him stop, freeze, look around to see where the danger might be, and then scurry off.

For the next three nights the same thing happened. We knew the neighbours were sick of this nightly glare on their bedroom windows, especially at 1am. We were also getting sick of seeing a red-eyed possum on our cameras and us as we rushed around the garden in our pyjamas at 1am. Maybe this time we were wrong and John was not the culprit. We decided to give it a few more days before we had the lights and camera removed.

It was as I was standing in the back garden looking at the plants pulled up and strewn over the lawn earlier – and I hadn't had the heart to clear up – that our neighbour from the house behind ours popped his head over our back fence and waved.

'Hi Lilli, I'm just fixing the palings in the fence here. I didn't want you to be alarmed when I started banging away.' I walked down to the back fence to see what it was about.

'See how the palings have come away from the fence here and here?' Our neighbour pointed to three palings that could be swung sideways, leaving a big enough gap for anyone to climb through. He grinned, with his mouth full of nails, as he pulled the first paling upright and grabbed a nail from between his teeth to begin hammering.

'Thanks Nigel, I hadn't even noticed this. How long has the fence been broken?'

'I don't know,' he replied. 'A few weeks I imagine as I haven't been down here in that time.'

I left Nigel hammering in the last nails and walked up the path to the back door. Now I knew how John had found his way into the garden. He had come via the house at the back. He must also have watched where the lights were when the possum had crossed the garden, and later chosen his path carefully.

We decided to cancel the sensor lights and camera immediately because we thought that once the palings were tightly nailed he wouldn't have this means of entry.

Nothing seemed to happen for a week or so. At first we were always on the lookout for more trouble – then we began to relax. Perhaps the sensor lights and camera had been effective and convinced him that we meant business.

We were still prepared to find new identities for Jenny and the kids.

My creative writing class had not met for a few weeks as it had been school holidays when no classes were held, but I was looking forward to the class resuming, hoping that one of my classmates might have found out how to get a new identity.

I remembered a few books I'd read about people changing their identities. I re-read them but they seemed to gloss over how to do it. Perhaps they didn't know either.

Still, I was aware that it could happen, as people did change their identities. It was witness protection people who most often seemed to be able to make the changes so that no one could find them. This was all done with the help of the police when witnesses to crimes were in life-threatening danger.

I would have loved to ask the police who had come to the house before how changing identity was carried out, but of course I couldn't ask. They probably knew all the scams that could be perpetrated by criminals changing their identities but would look suspiciously at me if I asked them about it.

My mind would not stop thinking about John. For short periods I would be busy shopping, or making dinner, and I would forget. Then all my tortured thoughts would envelop me again, causing an almost physical pain that seemed to come from my heart. I could understand now when people talked about being heart-broken, because that was the feeling I experienced.

Mac often sat in his chair with the TV remote in his hand. I could tell he was not watching whatever was on the screen. His mind was where mine was, thinking of John and Jenny, and feeling his own heartache.

One day I was at the meat section in the supermarket when I remembered a story about John and Jenny in happier times. It was a first visit to the newly-weds' unit. Jenny had spent some time deciding on the menu and had consulted me a number of times. I knew she was keen to show off the unit and her new cooking skills.

Tony and Samantha were invited too, and while Jenny was in the kitchen, John poured drinks for us all.

'This is so nice,' Samantha said. 'It's a pity your mum and dad aren't here too.'

John's reply was loud and clear.

'I'm glad my mum and dad aren't here in Australia. I like to live far away from interfering parents and in-laws.

Looking towards Jenny, he said, 'We'd rather be by ourselves.'

Samantha looked at me and raised her eyebrows. John just went on handing out drinks. I didn't know what to say or how to act. I felt that Mac and I should gather our gear and leave with a statement such as, 'Well, we'll leave you to it then.' But of course I didn't want to ruin Jenny's dinner and cause friction in the family. So we sat there, feeling unwanted, angry and impotent.

'Excuse me,' came a voice from behind me, and I realised I'd been standing at the meat section in a daze. I quickly moved to one side with an apologetic smile and then walked on. It seemed to me now that John had always wanted Jenny all to himself.

Chapter 13

'What do you want to drink, mate,' said the thin faced, squinty eyed barman. He looked quizzically at us as if we didn't belong there. And indeed we didn't. It was a run-down pub in Bondi that smelt like a brewery with the added aroma of sweat and fried food.

'A shandy and a middy of Peroni, thanks mate,' Mac said, handing over a note.

We had met Ray, an old school friend of Mac's, at a function and immediately Mac thought he might be able to help us. He had been a boxer in his early years and had won a prestigious bout, to become Australian Lightweight Champion.

After a rousing handshake and plenty of back slapping, we had coffee in a nearby café and while I sat and sipped my drink, Mac and Ray discussed who from their class was doing what, who was making money, who was divorced, who travelling or out of work.

'Ray, mate, I wonder if you can help us. We know someone who needs a new identity. It's legit. They're just being harassed and need out. You know … birth certificates, passports, licence etc. I guess I thought that the fringe element in the boxing fraternity might be of help.'

Ray laughed, his craggy face breaking into a wide smile.

'You mean do I know any pimps, con men, thieves and criminals from my boxing days?'

Mac looked ashamed.

'I didn't mean you. Just that you might have heard of someone …?' He trailed off and looked closely at Ray.

'As a matter of fact I do know someone, who might know someone, who could help you'.

Ray rubbed a finger against a nose that seemed to have been broken many times. 'I'll give you his name and how to find him.'

So here we were now, at this down-at-heel pub, to see a man who evidently knew someone, who knew someone else, who could get us forged birth certificates and passports.

We took our drinks and moved to a small table near the door. The table was sticky and the two ashtrays were full of butts that smelt terrible. I wrinkled my nose in distaste, but noticed a guy in a dirty overcoat watching me with a sarcastic look. I quickly looked down at the table and kept my head down.

We didn't fit in. Would the person we were meeting think we were genuine or would he think we were 'police plants' to get him 'nicked', as the customers of this pub might say?

Goodness! I was learning the vernacular of the area already.

Mac had been given instructions so that the man would recognise us.

We had to sit or stand near the door and wear something red. I looked around. Fortunately no one else was wearing red. I suppose this person knew that everyone would be in dull grey or brown.

Then a thin sallow chap in a red T-shirt under an old scruffy overcoat, and wearing a thin, dark blue, woollen beanie, slid into a seat across from us and, staring at Mac, asked him to shout him a schooner of VB.

Mac looked at me. He didn't want to leave me with this stranger. I elbowed him and nodded, to indicate that I'd be all right. Mac went off to get the drink while I stayed in my seat. I couldn't look at this criminal-looking man, so I kept my eyes on the table and sipped my drink. He didn't say a word until Mac returned.

Mac set the schooner in front of the man and then sat and sipped his own beer.

Eventually the man said, 'I'm Sol. What do you need?'

'We need a new identity for some people we know. Birth certificates, a licence, passports. Do you know someone who could help us out?'

'Maybe,' said Sol. 'If you've got some readies on you.'

'How much?' Mac asked, as he took another drink.

'Probably $10,000 for each identity and $1000 for me to find you the right person to do it.'

'Oh, no,' I gasped.

Sol just looked at Mac, never at me, and said, 'This doesn't come cheap, mate.'

'What do we have to do?' asked Mac.

'I'll talk to my mate and see if he'll do it. He'll need the money up front along with photos of the people, birth dates and your address. He'll probably change the birthdate and address just a bit so that it won't look too suspicious.'

Mac sat up taller, to seem more imposing.

'I'm prepared to pay half up front and the rest when we get the papers.'

'All right,' Sol said grudgingly.

'When do you want everything?'

'Meet me tomorrow, same place, same time and we can negotiate.'

'How do I know you won't take our money and disappear?'

'Well, you don't really. You'll have to take us on trust.' He smiled a nasty smile.

Mac made a quick decision. There was nowhere else to go. We had no other opportunities. We had to go along with it.

'Okay,' Mac said.

'Tomorrow night. Seven o'clock, right here.' We got up to go as Sol sat back and smiled. I didn't like the look of that smile at all.

Outside the pub Mac and I breathed deeply, from relief. We had just committed ourselves to $31,000. But Mac pointed out that the guy wasn't charging much for his own role in the service, provided, that is, he was telling the truth. We didn't know if we were being taken for a ride. But we hoped that it would save Jenny. That was all we could think of.

Back home, Mac transferred money from our share portfolio to the everyday account, ready to withdraw it the next day. I found photos of Jenny and the children that were suitable for a passport. Thank God I had so many because it took a while to find shots of them not smiling, the way the government insisted on passport photos these days. Mac and I went to bed, exhausted.

………………..

The pub was as dirty as the day before. I don't think they'd cleaned it at all. We sat in the same place with the same red shirt and scarf.

Suddenly Sol was there asking for a schooner, which Mac got him. Then we handed him half the money, the photos and information in a manila envelope. 'Under the table, under the table,' Sol growled as Mac started to hand it to him.

We watched our money disappearing into Sol's coat pocket. 'Come in a fortnight, same time same place,' he whispered and disappeared towards the back of the pub.

We left the table, weaving our way through a small crowd gathered near the door until we were outside in the fresh air.

'Got what you wanted?' called out a man sitting in the gutter with a cigarette in his mouth that smelt suspiciously like marijuana.

I don't even know. But maybe in a fortnight.

Our car careered off up the steep Bondi Road hill. Home seemed like another life away.

Two weeks later we set off for the pub again. We were very worried that no one would be there and we'd have just lost $16,000. We sat in the same seats and had the same drinks as before. Suddenly there was Sol in his dirty brown coat.

'Here you are,' he said, slipping the bundle of papers under the table. Mac copied his action of sliding them into his coat pocket. We exchanged the rest of the money. Outside once again, we jumped into our car and sped off, not game to look at the bundle before we'd left the area.

At home we opened the papers. There were birth certificates for Jenny, Chiara and Ryan. There was a passport with Chiara and Ryan on the same one as Jenny, and a driver's licence for Jenny. Their new names were Jackie Holloway, Chiara Holloway and Ryan Holloway.

This would be the beginning of a new life for them and for us too. We were so relieved. We would tell Jenny tomorrow, we decided. In the meantime, we locked the documents in the study desk and went to bed. For the first time in a long while we felt contented.

It wasn't until the early morning that we realised how wrong we were.

I was cold about 3am and needed another quilt. Gently, I touched Mac's shoulder. He was fast asleep and very warm. I contemplated just spooning up to him to get warm. Then I thought how I really did want some warm space for myself. So I padded down the hall to the linen press and hauled out a suitable quilt.

As I hurried back to bed I could feel a cold draught on my back. I looked at the hall window and saw that it was open. I was sure that I had closed and locked it the night before.

Gathering the quilt around me, I stepped over to the window to slide the panel to close it. It was then I saw a perfectly round hole in the glass where the draught was blowing in. I looked down at the window ledge and saw the nail that Mac had used to lock the window was lying on the ledge.

Someone had been in the house while we were asleep. They'd cut the window, opened it, climbed in, walked right past our sleeping forms and goodness knows what they'd done then.

I shook Mac awake.

'What's up?'

'Someone was in here or maybe still is. Mac, what will we do?'

Mac shot up from the bed and grabbed the nearest thing that could be used as a weapon. It happened to be our bedside lamp with a brass base.

We crept down the hall, both of us barefoot, and I was quaking, trying not to step on the lamp cord which was trailing behind him.

We searched every room, under the beds, in the wardrobe, in the shower and in the broom and linen cupboards. Nothing. No one. We went back to the lounge room while I told Mac about the window. If anyone was going to take anything, it would be in the lounge room where the computer, the TV and some precious ornaments were.

I looked around and then thought about the identity papers. They'd been locked in the roll top desk in the study, beside the closed-in back verandah. I signalled to Mac and we rushed down the hall. If someone had been in the study we wouldn't have heard them from the front bedroom.

Our worst fears were realised. The slats of the roll top had been forced apart with a knife, I guessed. Their shattered, broken edges stuck up from the desk like broken fingers. I peered down into the desk.

'Mac, the identity papers! They're gone.'

Jenny's chance of a new life has disappeared – along with our $31,000.

Chapter 14

'We're investigating a crime and you're a person of interest to us in this matter.'

The same imposing and frightening Sgt Ronson, who'd previously come to the door when we thought we'd been broken into, along with his athletic female partner, Constable Bailey, stood on our doorstep.

Their police car was angled across our driveway, the strobe light on the roof reflected in all our neighbours' windows. I imagined I could almost see all the curtains twitching as our friends peered out at such a sight.

With my heart beating at triple its normal rate, I opened the door wider to invite them in. We still looked sleepy-eyed as we'd been awake worrying for much of the rest of the night, only falling asleep in the early morning.

Mac joined me in the lounge room and we sat on the edge of our large comfortable lounge with our knees together and our hands in our laps. We felt far from comfortable. Children, sent to the headmaster, ready to be punished for talking in class.

'Could you answer some questions please,' Sgt Ronson asked, briskly refusing to answer Mac's enquiry of, 'What's wrong, officer?'

I just nodded. We were both still in shock over the loss of the identity papers and our $31,000, let alone having two police officers land on our doorstep to question us.

'Where were you last evening and night?'

Oh, no, no, no. My palms began to sweat and my throat felt as if it was closing up so that I could hardly breathe. They knew about us. I couldn't speak.

Luckily, Mac answered for us. 'We went to a pub in Bondi and then we came home and stayed here until we went to bed at about 11pm.'

'Can you confirm that with someone at the pub?'

Once again Mac answered for us. 'Well, the barman saw us and a man at the table where we were sitting would have noticed us and maybe he'd remember us. Otherwise I don't know.'

'Did you go to meet someone?'

'No,' Mac replied. I knew Mac was more frightened of Sol than the police. 'But we did speak to the man at the table while we were there.'

'What about?' Constable Bailey asked.

'Just chit chat,' said Mac. 'What's this about?'

'A man has been murdered in the lane beside the pub. He had your names and address on a piece of paper in his pocket. How did he get that information?'

We both sat there stunned. The officers stared at us. If they were hoping to see some guilt written on our faces, or a confession that we had murdered him, they were out of luck.

I could see out of the corner of my eye that Mac was trying to compose an answer which would seem sensible and real. I hoped that Constable Bailey didn't see his hesitation as a lie.

'We're thinking of selling our house and the man we chatted with was quite interested. He asked us for my name and address.' The answer seemed so flimsy to me and to Mac too, that to cover his hesitation, he straight away got up and asked them if they would like some coffee or tea. They both shook their heads.

'No thank you. Let's just go back through this again. When did you arrive at the pub?'

'Umm, I think about 5pm.' I had found my voice. 'Am I right, Mac?'

'I think so,' Mac replied, looking at the policewoman writing furiously in her notebook.

'What did you do first?'

'We went up to the bar and ordered a drink each from the bartender.'

'Can you describe him for us?'

'He was thin, with blond hair, and was about thirty years old. He had a grey T-shirt on with some writing on it. I couldn't tell you what it said. He had squinty eyes.'

The questions were coming faster now. I tried to collect my thoughts: *This is a way of making sure we don't lie, as we won't have time to make up answers without seeming to hesitate and correct ourselves all the time.*

'Where did you sit?'

'We sat near the door at a table.'

'Did you see anyone looking suspiciously at you, or anyone else who seemed suspicious?'

Mac grunted. 'Everyone in that bar looked suspicious to us.'

'Why were you there then?'

Mac and I looked at each other. Why were we there? What could we say that would make sense? I jumped in with an answer straight away.

'I needed to go to the ladies bathroom, and this was the closest pub we knew about. We thought we'd have a drink while we were there as well. After we settled in with our drinks we could see that it wasn't a very savoury place and we left as soon as we'd had our drinks.'

'Why did you speak to the man near you if you thought it was not a very nice place?'

'I don't know. Just polite, I guess.'

'Is this him?' Constable Bailey slid a photo in front of us. I gasped. It was Sol.

'I see you recognise him. Is this the man who sat near you?'

We both nodded, mute.

'How did the man behave? Did he seem frightened? Did he look around at anyone? Did you see anyone looking at him?'

Mac and I both shook our heads at each of the questions. Our answers didn't help the police at all. I hoped that our lack of knowledge about the pub and the people in it might end this interview.

'We might need some more information from you, so we may be back with some more questions,' Sgt Ronson said as he tucked his pen and notebook in his pocket.

'By the way,' Mac said. 'What was his name and how did he die?'

'Harmon,' Constable Bailey said. 'Sol Harmon. He was murdered. Executed with a single bullet to the head. Do you recognise that name?'

'No,' said Mac. I just shook my head. I could hardly speak. I cleared my throat several times as I ushered them back to the front door, before collapsing onto the lounge.

'What are we going to do?' was all I could think of.

'We can't tell them about Sol or they will want to know about the identity papers and then who they were for. It's probably a very big crime to have false identity papers, even though we don't have them anymore. But we did have them and we paid for them and who knows who's got them now, as it can't be Sol, he's dead and we'll never be able to ask him.' I'd rattled all this off in a scared voice, clutching at my hands and looking very guilty.

'Stop!' Mac broke into my monologue, grabbing me by the shoulders. 'You're getting muddled. Let's just think this through and then decide what to do. I don't like not telling the police what we know because it could help them find the murderer.'

I had a thought. 'What if it is John? What if he followed us to the pub? What if he asked someone what we were getting from Sol? What if he is listening to us now?' Mac and I rushed outside.

Mac stood silent for a minute. 'John can be pretty nasty but I don't think he would stoop to murder. It seems to me that the break-in was professionally done. The glass has been cut professionally. We heard nothing. Maybe they, whoever they are, were always going to take our money and then take back the identity papers for the next mug to come along'.

'I think it would be better to say nothing at all,' Mac continued. 'Whoever murdered Sol is probably a criminal, like Sol, and it is none of our business.'

I sighed. I hoped so.

The next morning two uniformed police officers arrived, spoke to us briefly, and waited outside in their police car for us to go down to the police station for an interview.

Mac and I sat in the back of the car while the two officers sat in the front. We could see the neighbourhood curtains twitching again, as nothing like this had ever happened in our quiet little street, where the residents were all honest and law abiding.

We had kept information from the police. We felt like criminals. We were criminals.

Chapter 15

We were ushered into a small, utilitarian interrogation room. It was painted a reassuring, soft peachy-pink colour, although the chairs were straight backed and hard, and the table was small, rocking a bit when I leaned on it.

I had read somewhere that this colour pink was meant to soothe people. The article said the colour was used by psychiatrists to put clients at ease.

It wasn't working.

We stuck to our story. Every time I felt troubled that we were not telling all, I thought about how Sol had probably intended to dupe us, how we didn't really know anything about the murder because we hadn't seen anyone watching or hanging around Sol in the pub, and that Jenny was our main concern.

Sgt Ronson showed us the picture of Sol again, for the record, and we were able to confirm that this was the man who asked for our names and address.

We felt very foolish when he inquired, 'Did you not think this was rather strange and that it might be a con?'

He stared at us with eyebrows raised that seemed to intimate that some seniors, that is us, were stupid. We repeated our story several times in different ways. We didn't add anything more to it. At one time they turned off the tape recording machine and offered us coffee or tea. We shook our heads and refused. They left us alone for about 15 minutes and I guessed that they were conferring outside about our story. My back was aching from sitting so straight and still for so long. I imagined how a real criminal would feel being in here. It was not pleasant.

Then we had to repeat our story again. We tried to stay calm and not get angry at this repetition. *Which is normal, to be calm or to be angry? Do we seem normal to them?*

Eventually, the interview ended, we were thanked and ushered out. I felt that the police officers were frustrated because they believed that we knew no more than we had said.

I wondered if we needed a lawyer. I didn't even know a lawyer who we could call. I'd have to find someone from the phone book. How would I know if they were any good at their job?

At home, we just slouched on the lounge chairs with the TV on. We were not watching it, not even noticing what was on. It was just noise in the background to dissipate our thoughts and to take away the stillness and quietness of the room.

We sat like this all afternoon letting the dusk roll over us and night descend. We didn't even turn on the lights. We only had the flickering glow of the TV. Every now and then one of us would whisper into the ear of the other, still aware that we might be bugged by John.

'What if someone saw us exchanging papers and money in the pub? What if a neighbour saw a person climbing in the window last night and the police come back to find out what happened? What if they look in our bank accounts and discover that $31,000 is missing on the same day that Sol is murdered? Will we have to put our house on the market, just so that we seem to be telling the truth about our statement?'

And then sometimes we whispered, 'Why would Sol give us the papers and then steal them. Why didn't he just take our money and run in the first place?'

Mac had an answer to that.

'I guess they wanted all the money, not just half of it. It's probably the way they operate all the time.'

We were both frightened. Frightened of criminals knowing where we lived; frightened of the police; frightened of going to prison; frightened that John would be listening and somehow make sense of what had happened and use it against us.

While we consciously knew the police were there to protect and serve us, there was a small subconscious part of us that became scared when we saw a police car behind us while driving, or when a knock came on the door. There was always this feeling that maybe we had done something wrong.

Years before, I'd also been a student at Alexander Mackie Teachers College in Paddington, near the law courts. During our lunch hour, some of us would go down to a courtroom to sit and watch the cases that were scheduled for that day, before going back to class. I had nightmares during that time that I was found guilty of a crime and imprisoned.

Mac and I were also both appalled that we could lie so well. We believed that we were law-abiding citizens. We had only ever nicked a few pens from our workplace or gone over the speed limit on country roads when there wasn't a camera around. We had never done anything really wrong. Now we were just like any criminal. We had tried to organise illegal identities; we had lied to the police, even if some of our falsehood was only by omission.

I was so dispirited that I couldn't think straight. I couldn't even get up to make dinner. It was fortunate that both Mac and I weren't hungry. We both felt that we would choke on any food, if we tried to eat.

I kept thinking about Sol. Had he been murdered for our money? We didn't know if he was murdered prior to someone breaking into our house or afterwards. Maybe he was murdered for other reasons. He certainly looked mean enough to have caused someone else to want him dead.

We stared at the flickering TV, filling our minds with its endless jumble of sound, when suddenly I happened to catch a few words that made sense. They were 'pub' and 'Sol.' It was the tail end of a breaking news story.

'A couple from a well-known criminal gang have been charged and remanded in custody for the murder of a man last night in a Sydney pub. Sol Harmon was shot once in the head, in an execution-style killing, and left in an alley near the pub in Bondi. It's thought that this was a murder between rival gangs. The police believe that the gangster-style killing was in revenge for stolen money.'

'Mac,' I whispered. 'Did you hear that?'

Mac grabbed the remote and immediately turned to another channel, hoping to hear that slice of news again. We heard it twice more on two different channels in exactly the same format. There was no extra information to be had. On one channel there was a picture of the pub and the inside area. There was also a picture of Sol.

The most reliable news channel, the ABC, gave us a little more information, a description of Sol. He was married and lived in Ashfield. He'd been an artist in his youth but had been jailed on a number of occasions for offences regarding forgery.

Mac and I fell back on the lounge. I cried with relief. We held each other and I could feel Mac's body begin to relax as mine slumped. It was over. We were no longer suspects. We believed that with charges laid against two people for the murder of Sol, we were in the clear. Even the word 'forgery' in the news bulletin didn't prompt any questions in our minds about the extent of any prosecution evidence that might be uncovered.

Now we believed all we had to do was figure out what our next move would be to help Jenny. It had to be one that didn't cost so much and was within the law.

We were not cut out to be criminals.

Chapter 16

We decided to visit the Hunter wineries as a way of forgetting the fright we'd had from the police over Sol's death.

Mac drove up the M2 motorway, turning off at Cessnock. This had been a major town in the days of coal fuel and was still rather quaint, with a great many pubs patronised by thirsty miners. Now it was the hub of the wine growing area, so there were posters and signs everywhere saying, 'NO MORE COAL SEAM GAS'.

After three hours in the car, we were glad to get out and stretch our legs at the first winery, Brayton's. All the wineries that were open for tasting had signs near their front gates, with winding roads bordered by trees leading up to the tasting sheds.

At first we drank from every glass that was offered to us, but after three wineries we became more selective and even rolled the wine around in our mouths before spitting it back into the glass. By lunch time we had had tastings at five wineries and bought a selection of wines ranging from whites, reds and muscats to sparkling wines.

The last winery named after the iconic racehorse, Phar Lap, had a café attached, and we decided to have lunch there at wooden tables overlooking the sloping fields filled with gnarled vines covered in fresh shoots of green.

It was a beautiful day and being mid-week there weren't too many people around.

Mac chose lamb focaccia and I had chicken risotto. It was served on large thick country plates accompanied by icy cold glasses of white wine. I was onto the dessert of blueberry cheesecake when I spotted someone I knew. She was gazing open-mouthed at me and then at Mac.

I nudged Mac. 'Do you remember that woman over there? I can't think of her name.'

Mac looked over and frowned. 'She's coming this way. We'll have to wing it.'

'Is it you?' the woman asked as she approached us tentatively, staring into our faces. I felt like saying, 'Yes it is us,' but I didn't. It seemed too rude when we couldn't even remember her name.

'I thought you were dead, but here you are looking well and hearty. I'm glad you survived the accident. When Bill told us about the lorry on the road, I remembered how we'd had a near crash several years ago and had just scraped by with no one hurt, although the car was a write-off just the same.'

'Anyway, how are you?' She seemed entranced.

I frowned at her breathless prattling. I wondered how to find out her name. If I could remember it, I was sure I'd remember where I knew her from. Then I thought she might have had us confused with someone else she knew.

'Which Bill told you?' I asked.

'Um, I think it was Bill Trilby from art class.'

Art class! It was then I remembered her name. Shirley.

'Well, Shirley, we are hale and hearty and I don't know how such a rumour got around about us. It's nice to see you again though.'

Shirley screwed up her nose.

'It must have been someone else and not you who had the accident, but I'm sure Bill said Lilli and Mac. We thought it was shocking that Mac would be accused of drink driving when we knew how careful he was. So … all the time it wasn't you, thank goodness. Oh, there's my friend waving to me. We're off to another winery so I guess I'll see you sometime around the art world. All the best, and bye for now.' She waved as she scurried away to join her friend.

Mac and I just looked at each other. What an amazing encounter! And fancy a rumour about Mac's driving. We needed to scotch that before it got around to everyone.

After that incident we set off home, abandoning the rest of the wineries. The case of wines we had bought rattled and clinked together in the boot and I was glad we'd had such a good beginning to the day, even if the last hour had been a bit of a shock.

I was determined to phone or email Bill when I got home to tell him we weren't dead.

Fiddling around on our computer looking for Bill's email address, I thought to check out Twitter.

And there was John in a large photo on the screen, looking at me.

John was on Twitter!

We were not very capable with social media forums and in fact we didn't know he was on Twitter. I scanned down the page and came across a diary section that John had written the day before. As I read it I became amazed to see that he had written about Jenny and the kids as if they were still with him.

Today we went to the zoo. Ryan loved the elephants and Chiara the monkeys. Jenny and I sat on the grassy slope nearby and looked out over the harbour. We will miss this when we go.

What was he doing? Was this written just the day before? And where would he go, I wondered? I looked at the date of the post. Yes, it was the previous day. I scrolled back through the last two weeks, certainly after Jenny had left, and discovered stories about John, Jenny and the kids each day. Obviously he was not admitting to anyone that Jenny had left him. In fact he was pretending that all was well and they were having fun. Weird!

Was this his way of keeping the fact that Jenny had left him a secret out of a sense of shame or was he trying to convince himself? Perhaps he'd gone out of his mind. I couldn't work it out.

Mac came over to the computer when he heard me catching my breath.

'What's up?'

I showed him the last month of John's diary, which must have been written after Jenny had escaped to Wolf's house. I wondered what else John had on social media. I looked for him on Facebook and found him. But we weren't friends of John so we couldn't access his page.

We abandoned the computer for a while and set out for our walk. I thought what a perfect day it was as we walked down to the golf course at Long Reef and along the boardwalk that led to Dee Why. There were a number of hang gliders at the top of the cliff enjoying the free rides to be had in the strong breeze. Mac and I sat on the bench nearby and watched them. They were so game. They could run to the edge of the cliff and just take off into space, confident that their equipment would keep them up in the air. Such a sense of freedom! Their lives were in stark contrast to Jenny's, I thought.

By now I was keen to speak to Jenny about John and Twitter. Maybe she'd have some ideas about why he'd do this. I held the phone between Mac and myself.

'Jenny, how are you?'

'Mum, it's so good to talk to you. Is Dad with you?'

'Yes, I'm here too, love. How are the kids?'

'Everyone's fine here, Dad. The kids are having fun. I think this move to Sydney has been good for them. Already they're spending much more time in Wolf's garden than where we were, getting lots of fresh air and not spending so much time watching TV or on the computer.

I told Jenny about Twitter and John's diary entries.

'What's that about?' I asked.

'I think John would think that I would look to see what he was doing and this is his way of still trying to control me. He would want me to think about how the kids would miss him and the good times we could be having. It's a bit like him saying, "I'm sorry, I won't do it again," after he's hit me.'

'Oh dear,' I said. 'Poor you. Well, now he can't hurt you anymore.'

We moved on to conversations about the kids and how she was getting on, coping with them at home every day alone, as well as talking over plans for the future. Afterwards we analysed her tone of voice and came to the conclusion that she was happier than we'd known her to be for a long time, even though she was facing the enormous constraint every day of being stuck in the one place with the children.

I couldn't resist looking on Twitter the next day to see if John had posted another story.

There it was! A new story about Jenny buying a beautiful dress and then both of them going to a famous Sydney restaurant while the kids had the girl next door baby-sitting. It all seemed so real. I clicked on the conversations page and scrolled through the people who'd been conversing with him. There were several people whose names I recognised from Jenny having talked about them, but most had a nickname or alias.

As I scrolled back over the last months of conversations, I noticed my name. It seemed to jump out at me as your own name often does on a page of writing, or when hearing people say your name in a crowd. My mind went blank as I read. How could he do this?

'Mac,' I whispered. 'Look.'

I read it again.

. Jenny's mother and father have been killed in a car accident. We received the news from the local police who were very sympathetic. Evidently they had been speeding along the M2 motorway and had tried to pass a large interstate lorry. They had miscalculated the distance and hit a truck coming in the other direction. Both of them died instantly as well as the truck driver. It was later discovered that Jenny's father, who had been driving, had an alcohol reading of 4.1 which explained the bad judgement.

A number of people that obviously knew John and Jenny as well as us, had responded to this post with condolences and questions about the funeral. John had replied, saying that the funeral would be private and only the family would be in attendance.

I thought about this. I guessed that none of our family or friends had seen this post as they, too, hadn't realised that John had a Twitter account. It seemed funny that not one of Jenny's friends had spoken to her about our deaths. Of course, her two best friends had been away on holidays and in hospital so maybe they hadn't had time for Twitter. Then I also remembered that for some time Jenny hadn't been allowed to talk to any of her friends when they rang. John always said she was out or sick and he would give her the message.

I scrolled forward several weeks and saw another post about us. Here, John was saying that Jenny had been left a significant amount of money by her parents and they were thinking of moving to Greece.

So, I thought. This was all part of a plan to cut off any connections with us and with Australia.

Chapter 17

'I wish you'd told me some details about what you were planning,' Jenny said. 'I would have stopped you, if I'd known. I thought you were just talking generalities. Mum, you need to leave this to me to sort out now. You've done all you can and I thank you, but leave it to me, please.'

I had put the phone on high volume so both Mac and I could hear Jenny. We'd decided to tell her what had happened with the identity papers and Sol's death, along with our police interrogation, just in case there were any rumours around the area that might reach her.

Jenny went on to introduce an unexpected development.

'In fact, I've been thinking I might take Jed up on an offer he made me this week. I've told him about John and the predicament we're in and he came back yesterday with an idea.'

'What idea?'

'His property in Victoria has a manager's house that's not used any more. It's about three hundred metres up the road from the main house where he's lived all his life. Now that his mum and dad are no longer alive, he's paid out his sister for her half of the property and lives there by himself. He said we could have the manager's house for free, until we sorted ourselves out.'

'What about Chiara? She'll need a birth certificate to start school in February,' I said.

'I've thought of that,' Jenny said. 'His sister, husband and niece have just recently moved to Adelaide and have left all their documents for safe keeping at the family home. They could come in useful for us.'

'How?' I asked.

'Jed's niece is about the same age as Chiara and he thinks he can copy the birth certificate on his computer, then cut and paste to change the name on it to Chiara, leaving the same surname as his niece, which is Heath. We don't think any school will be looking too intently at birth certificates for forgeries. Besides it's a two-teacher school with only twenty-two children in it. So I think the teacher will be too busy to take much notice, with all the things he or she has to do.'

Now my fear had turned to relief.

'That sounds like a good plan – and thank goodness you have somewhere to go because, you know, Wolf returns soon.'

'I've explained to Chiara and Ryan they'll be living in the country near Jed, where there are cows and horses and dogs. And I've also told Chiara that she'll be going to a nice little school. They're looking forward to the move.'

'What about John? Don't they ask where their dad is?'

'At first they asked a lot, but now it's less and less. Occasionally Ryan asks, and seems satisfied with my answer that he's overseas. Chiara's a different matter. She's old enough to wonder what's happening.'

'Poor little thing. What do you say to her?'

'I tell her that Daddy lives overseas now for his work. Sometimes she cries at night because she misses him, but mostly she accepts what I tell her. We have lots of cuddles to keep her mind off it.'

Mac and I glanced at each other. We both thought this idea of Jed's might save the day for us and Jenny. We could only hope that Jenny was making the right decision. It would certainly be far away from John, and Jed had seemed a quiet, responsible fellow to me.

It was a beginning to feel like a load off our minds.

Over the previous week – since the police enquiries about Sol and his murder and the theft of the identity papers – we hadn't seen the Mazda around, or had any harassment from John. Perhaps he'd given up his revenge. But we'd keep up the charade when we talked about Jenny because we were nervous that the bugs could still be in the house.

Early the following week we had a good laugh with our neighbours about the police coming to the house and asking us about a man who'd been murdered. Life seemed to be back on an even keel.

And Christmas time was coming. We decided it was too soon to visit Jenny and the kids in case we were followed, but I was determined to make their day exciting and fun from a distance. I shopped for all the little things that I knew they liked. For Jenny, I decided to make a photo book of her early life before she'd met John, to remind her of who she was and how lovely she was. I was able to post off to Wolf's house small parcels at different times, so that John, if he was still watching us, wouldn't suspect that we were sending things to Jenny.

But the following week the harassment started again. This time, though, it didn't concern us as much as before, I guess, because we'd already had a fright over possibly being jailed for murder. Each week there was some new thing that let us know that John was still around and still believed that we had something to do with the disappearance of Jenny and the children. It might be all our letters torn into pieces and strewn on the ground. Sometimes it was rubbish thrown onto the verandah. But no one in our street ever noticed him doing any of this.

Mac and I were more concerned that he could hack into our computer and take our savings. We reduced our Visa card so that only $500 could be taken out at any one time. We also changed our password every week. As well, we arranged for the bank to pay funds into Jenny's new account on a regular basis. And we never used the internet to make payments from home.

Feeling increasingly fidgety, I decided to clean the house from top to bottom. It would keep my mind busy, I decided. It was while I was doing this that I came across a bug in the lounge room. It was about as big as my thumbnail and was stuck in the corner of the bookcase. At first I didn't know what it was. I was turning it over and over in my hand with a frown on my face when Mac came to the door.

'What's up?' he asked.

I showed him the gadget. 'Is this something of yours you want to keep?' I asked.

'That,' said Mac, 'is a bug.' He grabbed it and trod on it until it was in pieces, as if it was a real insect-type bug. I looked horrified. We had thought there were bugs, but this was the first real proof.

Mac strode over to the phone and rang the security company we had engaged for the door codes and security cameras.

They agreed to come straight away, and, after confirming that it definitely was a bug, and we paid them the exorbitant fee of $475, they set about searching for bugs in all the other rooms of the house, using a complex and technical piece of equipment.

In all there were four bugs found, including the bug I'd found in the lounge room: one in the bedroom, one in the study and one in the kitchen. All places where we might talk about Jenny.

They were most interested to uncover why we might have bugs in our house and when we muttered vaguely that we didn't know why, they suggested we phone the police straight away as this was a matter of privacy abuse.

'It's unlucky that it's only a sound camera because it makes it difficult to find the perpetrators. If it had been webcam with pictures, we could have traced it back to the place where the information is being uploaded.'

'Yes, that's very unlucky,' I agreed, all the time thinking that I'd rather have a sound camera than webcam showing what we did at home each day.

The security company also suggested that we get a sweep of the house every month for security purposes. We wondered whether we could afford to do that every month, although it would have relieved our minds somewhat. But John could replace the bugs a day after they had been removed and we mightn't even have known. We decided to carry on talking outside as we were doing now.

Finding the bugs though, lessened our anxiety somehow. It seemed as if knowing we were right and John was the culprit caused us to feel more confident that we were on top of things.

We suspected that John would get angrier with our discovery of the bugs. What would he do next? What could he do that he hadn't already done? If the worst came to the worst, we could sell the house and move, possibly into a gated community. We consoled ourselves with this plan, even though it seemed extreme.

I asked Mac again if he thought we should phone the police. After much discussion we decided that we couldn't do it. The police would only ask why we thought we were being bugged. It might also open up an investigation into Sol's murder again and we'd both be viewed as people to watch – 'persons of interest'.

Let's not rock the boat, we decided.

Chapter 18

It's funny how things happen.

Sometimes, if I think about a star of yesteryears, stage and screen, I then see a movie about that star on midnight TV a few days later. If I wonder what happened to that famous tennis champion, there he is in a documentary the next week. If I talk about the author of a book I'm reading, there she is on the front page of the *Manly Daily* celebrating her 92nd birthday.

I always wonder if I can conjure up events and people with my mind, but usually Mac and I laugh at this coincidence. 'Spooky,' we say and let it go at that.

It was while I was doing the Manly Daily crossword one afternoon that an advertisement for a lecture on domestic violence caught my eye. I read the whole section. There was an expert on child abuse coming to the Dee Why RSL to speak about domestic violence and the effect it had on families. I wanted to know more.

'Hey, I want to go to this,' I told Mac. 'It may help us to understand what's happened to Jenny and the children.'

Mac saw that it was the following Saturday afternoon and immediately booked us two seats.

The theatre room at the RSL was packed. There were a great many women and a scattering of men. Some of them looked to be groups from various clubs, come for a lecture and an outing at the RSL. A few looked very pale, bleak and sad. I wondered if these were people who were experiencing violence at home and had come for help.

The lecturer was about forty years old. She looked kind and was dressed in a smart casual outfit that wasn't too official-looking. I supposed that the informality of her clothing was aimed at creating a bond between herself and her audience.

She began by telling us about different types of abuse, such as sexual, medical, physical, domestic and mental. I hadn't realised that there were so many kinds and how prevalent it was in the community.

When she talked about domestic violence, she said that most violence was perpetrated by men, although some women were violent too. There were many reasons why people became violent, including early life issues, lack of control, a need to dominate and a belief that women were servants to men.

I looked at Mac. We were both thinking of John's early life and how maybe something that occurred back then could have affected his behaviour.

She mostly explained how we might recognise that abuse was taking place and what we could do about it as citizens.

'Abused women often wear long-sleeved shirts even on very hot days. They might wear scarves around their necks so that bruises can't be seen. They might appear frightened or cowed a lot of the time and often react violently to loud noises or sudden movements such as another person raising their arms,' she said.

I thought about Jenny. She had not told us she was having any trouble at home, although she had appeared very quiet and subdued over the past few years. We mostly hadn't noticed these changes, or if we had, at the time we had said nothing.

It was when the speaker went on to talk about how domestic violence might affect children that I sat up to take notes.

The lecturer said that most domestic violence included loud shouting and noisy fights as well as physical abuse. Sometimes it was perpetrated by controlling the wife, not allowing her to have any freedom. While one might think that the children would not be aware of domestic abuse, they always were. Often they hid under the bedclothes in their room with a pillow over their heads to stop the noise of the fight. Little ones often cried themselves to sleep. Older children sometimes took sides with the female victim and showed hatred for the male perpetrator. This might cause the male to lash out more at the female, believing that she had turned the children against him. Sometimes children turned against the female victim believing that she was weak and not standing up to the male. Always their schoolwork suffered along with their relationships with other children. Either they felt they could not bring any friends home or they became loners. Teenagers often left home and did not finish their schooling. The spiral effect of this could be homelessness, no job skills, no friends, becoming emotionally stunted, and often addiction to drugs or alcoholism, and even suicide.

Mac and I sat there stunned. I had started to take notes but had given up after a few words as it was all too complicated and too much to take in.

We staggered out of the theatre, grabbing all the brochures and help material we could find on the table near the door. We went down to the café on the ground floor of the RSL and I burst into tears. How could this happen in our society? We were a country of plenty weren't we?

After a coffee, I felt stronger. Jenny was safe and away from such harm. She was in control of her own life again. The children were safe too. They were only little and there had been more verbal and mental abuse than physical. They hadn't seemed to be noticing anything. They still wanted to see their daddy. It seemed that we had been able to rescue Jenny and the children before any great harm had come to them.

I began to feel better. I began to feel that we had done the right thing in taking Jenny away from her home, even though at times I had been unsure.

We sat at the table and spread the brochures out. There were a couple that had headings such as 'What to do when you experience domestic violence' and 'Getting legal advice'. They interested us the most. Should Jenny go to one of the women's refuges in the area for help or seek legal advice?

We needed to talk to Jenny.

That afternoon we went for our walk and phoned her on the mobile.

'Jenny, love …' Mac used a soothing voice. 'We've just been to a very informative program that touches on what you have been through.'

Mac summarised the points from the lecture that might be helpful to Jenny. He mentioned that we had brochures on refuges and legal advice. I could hear Jenny murmuring as he spoke.

Then she said, 'I don't want to go to a refuge, Dad. I know it could help some people, but I've already left and have successfully hidden myself away, so far. They couldn't do anything more to help. As for legal advice, I would like this but I am unsure. What if the legal team say I must meet with John in a court case? What if he finds out where I am? What if he takes his revenge? The police haven't been able to protect you from his revenge. How would it be with me? Besides I don't want him to have anything to do with the children. He is too violent. And his violence might turn on them eventually.'

We listened to Jenny. It was really her decision. A little bit of me wanted her to take the legal route, but the biggest part of me felt that she was right.

At home we did some routine tasks. I watered the garden with most of my mind on the difficulties other people faced with abuse. At last I came to the conclusion that while John was harassing us, he probably had no time to find Jenny. This was a good thing and we could put up with this harassment while Jenny and the children were safe.

I went inside after a while to find Mac sitting in his chair watching the news. He seemed very tired and looked rather red in the face. I went over and held my hand against his forehead. It was very hot. I brought him a glass of water and a Nurofen. It was important to keep Mac's blood pressure from rising. What we had just learned would surely raise anyone's blood pressure.

I was worried.

Chapter 19

'There he goes,' I said as I peered out of the front windows and saw the blue Mazda go by for the first time in ages.

Suddenly the prepaid phone buzzed and jiggled on our bedside table. I picked it up and went out the front.

'Mum, I need your help.'

'What's wrong, love?'

'Ryan's sick. He was playing in the garden at Wolf's and was bitten on his arm by something. I think it was one of those white cross spiders that hide in leaves. Now he is crying, and the place where he was bitten is red and swollen. I need to take him to the hospital. Jed's in the city at a meeting and won't be home for hours. I'd get a taxi but I haven't got enough change and the last time I used the card it didn't work for some reason. I hadn't got around to telling you … '

'We'll be there as soon as we can.'

We rushed to lock up the house and started the car. We were headed for Jenny's place, but how were we going to avoid the blue Mazda?'

Mac started to drive along a new route to Wolf's house. I kept a lookout for John. At first there was no sign of a blue Mazda, but soon I saw John following three cars behind. At least I thought it was John. There were so many of them on the road.

Mac had a plan.

'I'll pull over and let you out at that block of flats up ahead. You go in the entry as if you are visiting someone. I'll carry on, hopefully without John, to Jenny and the hospital. I hope he thinks you are visiting Jenny there.'

It was all we could think to do. I jumped out without looking towards the Mazda, and entered the flats via the front double glass doors. There was a row of boxes in the foyer with names and buzzers. I pretended to be looking for the one I wanted, while I kept an eye out for any movement outside. The Mazda had stopped across the road. I could see it through the glass doors. How was I going to seem to be visiting someone? John could see into the foyer and would notice if I lingered there too long. I surreptitiously pressed several buzzers next to one another, hoping that one of the owners would buzz open the security door to the lift well. A voice from the intercom said, 'Yes?'

'Pizza,' I replied frantically. This always seemed to work on television.

'Didn't order one,' came the voice, and hung up.

There was nothing else to do. I hoped that Mac would be far enough away by now. I opened the doors and stepped into the street. Out of the corner of my eye I saw a man in the driver's seat of the Mazda turn towards me. I couldn't make out who it was because the car's windows were tinted. But I just knew it was John. The Mazda screeched off down the road.

I had fooled him! Even so, I waited about twenty minutes before I called Mac. I didn't want to interrupt him to cause any delay. Then I phoned Mac. Jenny and the children were with him in the car on the way to the hospital. He put the mobile on speaker and I checked how Ryan was. I boasted about my clever acting. I was jubilant. I was jubilant I'd thrown John off the scent.

They were nearly at the hospital. I felt innately that little Ryan would be all right. Those white cross spiders could make you very sick, but they were not fatal like redbacks or funnel webs, I thought. At least I hoped they weren't fatal for small children.

I considered going straight home, but I wanted to see Ryan and give him a hug. Surely John would go back to our place or his home. So I could catch a taxi to the hospital.

....

Ryan was sitting up in bed in Emergency with a big grin on his face. He was getting lots of attention from two nurses, as well as Mac, Jenny and Chiara.

His reddish curls fell over his forehead and his blue eyes peeked out at me.

'Nanna,' he crowed reaching out for me with two chubby hands. I hugged him close. I was reminded that it was that same 'Nanna' I had heard from Ryan, which had alerted me to the whole situation. I covered his face with kisses until he said 'Ugh' and wiped his cheeks with a glint in his eyes. He then showed me his spider bite.

I looked closely at the swelling. He was very proud of his bravery.

'We can go home any time now,' Jenny announced. 'The nurses don't want a little boy roaming their hallways.'

She was so light-hearted now, in contrast to the panicky mother I'd heard on the phone. She started to dress him and put on his shoes.

Chiara looked bored and a bit envious of all the attention on Ryan.

'Jenny, why don't you take Chiara to the vending machine at the end of the corridor to find a chocolate bar for her?' I trickled a few coins into her hand.

I had just finished tying Ryan's shoelaces when Jenny burst into the room.

'We've got to go …' She was breathless. 'An old friend of John's, George, is coming up the stairs. Because he and John work in IT, they might bump into each other and he could say he saw us at the hospital.

Jenny started to shake and Mac took charge.

'Put on this jacket of mine and my peaked cap. Pick up Ryan and go to the lifts in the other direction. I'll take Chiara.'

He quickly pulled a sheet from the end of the bed and covered her, hurrying from the room with a flick of his head to me to come with him. I grabbed a blanket, covered my head and shoulders with it and ducked out towards the lift, although I don't suppose George would have known me.

We couldn't look back. Jenny was busy pushing the lift button over and over again. The lift was taking its sweet time. At last it arrived and the doors opened.

We tumbled in and Mac pressed the button for the ground floor. As we stood there, looking out into the hallway, the doors seemed to close so slowly. I spied George's head come to the top of the stairs just before the lift doors closed.

We'd made it.

Chapter 20

The next day I woke with a feeling of contentment, knowing Jenny had not only avoided a head-on confrontation with John at the hospital but that she was on her way with Jed to the safety of Victoria. It was a new day and I was determined to make sure John didn't rule our lives.

The sun shone through the trees around the deck and we decided to have breakfast there. I made mushroom omelettes with crusty bread on the side. Tumblers of freshly squeezed orange juice added to the feast. After I'd arranged a white linen cloth on the deck's small table, I called Mac. The weather had been warming up over the last few days and a soft breeze swayed the trees.

A band of raiders, five lorikeets, came swooping down and landed on the rail. Their beady eyes looked at our food. We'd given up feeding the birds after a specialist on TV had spoken about the irresponsibility of feeding natives. Evidently the birds would become dependent on our scraps and lose some of their ability to forage for themselves.

After the chattering noise from the five of them, another five descended. I wondered how they knew what delicacies were at hand and realised that they must be talking to each other. It amazed me that their voices could be heard and interpreted over a distance as the second lot of birds hadn't been close.

Mac and I reluctantly fed them a few scraps from our crusty bread and then with a, 'That's all folks,' gathered our plates and moved inside. Within minutes they had flown away.

Later that day Wolf returned from Germany. We met him at his house and I saw at once that Jenny had left the place in a sparkling clean condition, with a thank you card on the table. There was a photo of Ryan and Chiara on the front.

I ran my fingers over it. I had only seen the children once since we had rescued them. They had grown in the last few months. The photo showed Ryan standing with a mud pie in his hands. Mud also adorned his t-shirt and jeans, and most of his face and hands. A cheeky smile peeped out from the mud. Chiara stood partly behind him with a rolling pin and wooden spoon in her hands. She was laughing at the camera and poking out her tongue. My heart melted and tears settled at the corner of my eyes. Mac, knowing how I felt because he felt the same, handed me his handkerchief. I sniffed and tried to smile, but noticed that his eyes looked a bit red rimmed too.

I'd brought over some delicacies for a light lunch on the bayside near the Palm Beach ferry, hoping it would restore our spirits and be a way of saying thank you to Wolf. So after our greetings, and with Wolf babbling about his trip, we drove over to Palm Beach for a picnic followed by a short walk.

The area near the ferry was part of Barrenjoey, first inhabited by the Garigal clan of the Gurungai-speaking aboriginal people who died out during a smallpox epidemic. In 1900 all the land was divided into eighteen large blocks and listed as good grazing land for sale. None sold. So in 1912 it was again offered as residential smaller blocks and was bought by people wanting a second holiday home. Now, of course, most houses were worth $2-6 million each. I wished my parents had bought a block there and I'd inherited it.

It was about fifty minutes later that we parked in the ferry carpark. The road had narrowed to a thin sliver of land with the beach on one side and the bay on the other. At the tip of the land was a lighthouse that had been there since early convict times. In our younger years, Mac and I had climbed the hill to the lighthouse and now we could see there were several young couples doing the same today. I recalled the view from the top as spectacular, a vista of sand, sea, trees and expensive houses sprinkled between.

I had mentioned to Mac several weeks ago that there might be an opportunity to meet with Jenny and the kids in a remote place like this. I had looked at him hopefully. Mac had frowned.

'I don't think it's a good idea. We never know when the blue Mazda will turn up. It would be a pity to ruin things at this stage.'

I'd had to agree with him.

The picnic basket was filled with delicious goodies. There was salmon on little pikelets with crème fraiche and dill, pastries with lamb curry, and cheese and olive tarts. I'd also brought a cheesecake with fig and Marsala syrup, and topped it all off with a bottle of rosé.

The three of us sat on a bench near the water, looking out at the boats moored in the bay. The ferry tooted and people waved at us as it left the wharf and turned towards the open water. We waved back.

I nudged Mac. 'Look at those black clouds. I think we're in for some rain.'

Mac and Wolf gathered our gear, while I packed up the remains of the food, but before we could get to the car, the rain poured down in a torrent of big wet drops. Within minutes we were soaked.

Mac fumbled for the keys and clicked on the remote. We all slid in with our wet bags and brushed some of the water off our clothing.

Mac started the car. Something was wrong. The car screeched forward as if it were in pain. Mac and I sat there for a moment, but Wolf immediately opened the car door and slid out. We didn't want to get out in the rain as well to see what was wrong, and Wolf straight away noticed a flat tyre.

'It's a flat,' he shouted, grimacing. 'Up the front here.'

I knew how draining it was to change a tyre but I got out to offer some support. Then I noticed that the back tyre on the same side was also flat. I walked around to the other side. All four tyres were flat.

This was too much of a coincidence. It must have been done on purpose.

'John!' I said.

I looked around but with the rain so heavy I couldn't see anyone who looked like John, or a blue Mazda. We would have to call the NRMA as we had only one spare tyre in the boot. The outing for Wolf's homecoming had been ruined.

We sat in the car while the rain pounded down. Eventually the downpour stopped as if it had never been. Mac slid out and started to walk towards the bonnet.

As we waited the obligatory hour for the NRMA to turn up, Mac told Wolf most of the story about Jenny and John. Then he turned to me.

'See, what did I tell you? We can never be sure that John won't be following us.'

Wolf was most sympathetic. Go to the police was his answer.

I wondered what would have happened if we'd gone to the police in the first place when we couldn't find Jenny and the kids. I ran it through my mind.

John would have said she'd left him and the police would have been satisfied. If Jenny had told them about John's abuse, he would have just denied it and might have taken his revenge on her. If we'd told the police John was hounding us and abusing Jenny, again he would have just denied it, the police would have had no proof and John would still have taken his revenge on us. We would have ended in the same predicament as now.

'What happened here?' the NRMA fellow asked when he saw four flat tyres.

Mac and I could only shrug and say it must have been kids. He had bought three tyres with him and was happy to have Mac and Wolf assist him in changing all four of them. He chatted as he did so. He was such a genial fellow and we were grateful for his help.

The ride home was uneventful. We kept a lookout for the blue Mazda on the road but really thought that John would have left Palm Beach long before we discovered the flat tyres.

Would we ever be free of him? Would we continue to be afraid that wherever we went, he might be there ready to do damage to us or our property?

I didn't know if I could stand it much longer.

Chapter 21

I took a sleeping pill that night.

Before I drifted off to sleep I consoled myself with a positive thought about Jenny. She'd told us that in making the decision to go to Victoria to live on Jed's property, she expected it would be for good. He was the kindest, most considerate man she'd met, she said, and handsome as a bonus. Mac and I had waited to be convinced, and now we both appreciated the kind of supportive practical man he was. It would all work out well, I just knew it.

And now we'd be able to reduce our financial support to Jenny – not that we wanted that consideration to have any bearing on her decision-making, we made that clear.

In the morning I woke up refreshed, without the knots in my stomach that I usually had. It was the first time in ages that I'd wanted to really face the day. I turned over to Mac and he pulled me across the sheet towards him. We cuddled and whispered loving words, in between soft little kisses, just as we'd been doing for all thirty-seven years of our marriage.

We belonged to an era that set an expectation of marriage for life. It wasn't like today where people marry knowing they can get out of it, if it's too hard. We felt that this option resulted in people not trying hard enough to make their marriage work. But what about people like Jenny?

We couldn't blame her. In fact, we felt that she was right to leave her husband.

With one last kiss, I rolled out of bed to make breakfast.

The day was warm, not like the sticky heat of January. Surely life would go right for us now. I hoped John would give up harassing us. Little did I know that life was just about to change for the worse!

The phone rang and Mac reached for it. It was Tony. He'd had three days off work but was still doing a few jobs from home.

'Dad, have you seen the blog about you on the internet?'

'No, what blog? And what exactly is a blog anyway?' He raised his eyebrows as he glanced at me. I nodded back, knowing that our children thought we were completely ignorant about computer-language.

'A blog is a program where you can put anything about yourself or your business online. People can go online and leave comments for you as well.'

'What's that got to do with us?'

'I was googling to check how common our surname, McGregor, is when a blog about you popped up. It's got big pictures of the two of you and a story that is so shocking and so defamatory that I had to phone you straight away.'

'Just a minute,' Mac said. 'I'll put the computer on and look myself.' I stood behind him and watched the screen light up.

'What do I put in to find it?'

'Just google your name.'

Mac googled his name and up came a whole page of writing, along with our photos. They were horrible. Whoever had taken these photos had caught us in horrible poses. I was bending over to get in the car and my dress had ridden up. The close-up honed in on my behind. Mac had been lifting something and the photo had caught him grimacing as he did so. We read the words underneath:

Lilli and Mac McGregor look like normal people in the suburbs. Don't be fooled. You can see Lilli's obese form shows her slovenly appearance and is a measure of her slovenly attitude to life. People who know her say she is a dirty housewife and smells when you get up close to her. As for Mac, his grimace shows you just how violent he really is. Keep clear of him if you live nearby as he could grab your children and hurt them.

'Are you there, Dad? Have you read it?' Tony asked.

'Yes,' said Mac hoarsely. 'What does it mean? Who could do this to us?'

It's called trolling,' said Tony. 'It's a form of cyber bullying. It's used to get an emotional response from the person being trolled. Anyone can put up a blog and write what they like.'

'Can we stop it?'

'Usually the cyber bully is anonymous. They have hidden their pathway so you can't find them,' Tony explained. 'I suggest you phone the police and see what they can do.'

Mac and I looked at each other, so I decided to say something to add a bit of support.

'John – with his IT knowledge, he's skilled enough to do this in revenge. We were wrong to think he's given up. It was too good to be true. We should call the police.'

Mac could only agree.

………………..

The same two police officers, Sgt Ronson and Constable Bailey, came to the door. I felt a bit embarrassed, thinking we must have had a red cross on our police file by now to let them know we were nuisances who had phoned many times over small annoyances. It might also say we could be liars.

Now we explained why we'd called them again, and showed them the blog on our computer. They noted the web name and took some notes about the site. Then we sat in the lounge room while they asked us some questions.

This time, although we sat on the edge of the lounge with our knees together and our hands in our laps, we did not feel like children in trouble. Rather we were adults needing police protection and help.

During our childhoods, we'd both been told by our parents that if a stranger came near you or anyone tried to hurt you, to run to the nearest policeman for help. But we'd also been told that if we were naughty, the police would get us. What mixed messages we were served up. No wonder we didn't know how to behave so many years later when the police came to the door.

'Do you know anyone who would do this?' Sgt Ronson asked.

'Yes, definitely,' said Mac.

It was the first time we'd confessed so easily that we thought we knew who had done it. Mac continued.

'We think it's our son-in-law. He came to our house because his wife, our daughter, had left him. He was very angry and said it was our fault and he would 'get' us. Since then we've had lots of harassment from him. You may have seen our file that shows how many times we've called you about strange happenings.'

Constable Bailey looked back through her folder. It was quite thick. It probably held reports on all the incidents that had happened to us.

'This is a very serious situation. The police are trying to eradicate this type of bullying. We'd like to take your computer with us and get our tech officers to try and find the person or persons who did this.'

'Okay,' said Mac and started to unplug the mainframe.

After they'd gone, Mac phoned Tony to tell him what had transpired.

'I hope they can do something,' Tony said. 'I've just looked at the blog again. It's only been a few hours and already there are new pornographic photos of each of you. They are obviously doctored photos that have your heads cut and pasted onto naked bodies but all the same they're very smutty.'

There was nothing we could do but rely on the police to come up with an answer. We went to the library to use their computers as we didn't have one now and probably would not have one for a while. I googled 'trolling'. Up came a vast amount of information.

There was a definition of trolling. Evidently it had been around for some time but had peaked globally in the last year, mostly due at first to angry young people who were unhappy with the state of their lives, unable to find paid work, feeling exploited and without hope for the future. Then it had been taken up by adolescents at school who were keen to cyber bully others.

There were also statements from parents who wrote about their teenagers' experiences with trolling. Some had even reported that their kids had tried to commit suicide or actually had committed suicide because of the nastiness and invasiveness of the trolling.

Parents and teachers were organising campaigns in schools to warn youth about the hidden dangers of social networks. Celebrities were often trolled, as were politicians. In fact it seemed like fair game to be doing this.

No one seemed able to catch the offenders or stop it spreading.

Chapter 22

'I've seen that blog about you and I don't believe a word of it.'

My neighbour Jean had crossed the road to speak to me, and my neck and cheeks were red with embarrassment as I had just seen the ugly photos and script that had appeared on the blog that morning.

'Thanks, Jean. I don't know who's doing it or why. It's very distressing. If I knew who it was, I'd kill them.'

I suddenly thought how that sounded and how it would sound in a court of law. I was always suspicious now of how the words and content that I spoke might appear to other people, and usually I was careful of what I said.

'We talked about the blog,' Jean said, 'and we've decided that we wouldn't look at it anymore. That's the best way of addressing it. If no one looks at it, it will go away.'

I smiled at her and waved goodbye as I drove off to the shops, wondering who the 'we' was. Probably all my friends and neighbours. I guessed we were the talk of the street.

I didn't think it would go away – especially if it was John's work, as I suspected. There was a number at the bottom of the blog that told everyone how many hits it had received. So far it was up to 29,000.

I noticed people at Warringah Mall looking strangely at me. I felt they were checking me out and wondering if I was the one they'd seen on the blog. I was almost at the stage of not wanting to go out anywhere.

Mac felt like that too. He was still going to bowls but had stopped going to the pub afterwards with his mates. He, too, felt everyone was looking at him. Maybe we were imagining this, but whether it was true or not, this was how we felt and we knew it was exactly how John would want us to feel.

We wondered how we could get to John and stop him. The police phoned after a week to arrange a time to deliver our computer back to us. They hadn't found a pathway to the origin of the blog. They didn't have any proof that the trolling was by John and were unwilling to search for him when there was no proof that he was the culprit.

One morning, I suddenly remembered about 'Lisa' in London. When we'd phoned John's parents, his mother had mentioned a 'Lisa' who had been in hospital. She'd said, or so I thought, that Lisa had been beaten by John. Maybe it was just my faulty memory about the abuse because of Jenny's abuse. Maybe I was wrong. I needed to know.

Could we find her and get some statement from her that would encourage the police to see John as a person of interest?

So we called John's parents again. I explained what was happening to us and asked them if they had Lisa's last name, phone number or address. John's mother admitted she had an address, only because she felt that she had needed to apologise to Lisa for John's actions. This seemed to confirm that he had abused Lisa in some way. I thanked her and took a deep breath before I phoned Lisa. She answered the phone on the second ring.

'Lisa Turnbull'.

'Hello, Lisa. My name is Lilli McGregor, phoning from Australia. We're concerned about a person called John, John Stanford, and we know from his mother that you had been going out with him. John Stanford married my daughter Jenny and we have had a lot of worries about him. Would you be happy to speak with us? Can you tell me what happened to you?'

I'd wondered whether Lisa would agree to speak with me. Taking a strange call from strange people in another country would not be something I would do. I'd hang up immediately, thinking it was a crank call.

That's exactly what she did. Dead air. I immediately phoned again but the phone was engaged. I was sure she'd taken the phone off the hook. I knew I could not pursue this avenue.

It seemed that not only had we needed to help Jenny get away from John, now we also had to find a way of avoiding his abusive behaviour towards us. The harassment and stalking that had gone before now seemed mild compared to this trolling.

We'd rung Jenny on her prepaid mobile as soon as she'd arrived on the farm in Victoria, using our mobile phone while on a walk. Jed had done as he'd said he would and arranged a very pleasant, if basic, place for her to stay on the farm. We wondered how long it might take before she moved into the big house, and I figured Jenny and Jed were just giving each other some space to adjust at this early stage.

Jed was proving to be a good friend to Jenny regardless of how long they might be lovers. He'd arranged for Jenny to live in the manager's house which was only three hundred metres or so from the main house where he lived. He could watch over her but still allow Jenny and the children to have a sense of autonomy. He'd arranged to hire a car which was transferred back to Sydney when they arrived in Victoria. He had thought this was best so that there was no evidence of air or bus tickets in Jenny's name. There was some relief in this for us too.

'Mum, my place has two bedrooms, a lounge/dining area, a kitchen and a bath/laundry,' her voice had trilled down the phone. 'The kids have their beds in the same room and love it. They have the paddocks of the property to run around in, although I won't let them go near the vealers. They're such big animals.'

'How are you?' I asked her.

'I'm all right at present. I feel a lot better now that we're away from Sydney and the possibility of John finding me. Jed has been really good. He is such a nice man, Mum.' I could hear a warm intensity about Jed in her voice.

'What about Chiara going to school in February?' I asked.

'Yes, we do need a birth certificate for her to start school in Victoria. So Jed is looking into it this week.'

I debated with myself about telling Jenny about the blog. But I thought better of it. There was no point in distressing her and it was unlikely she would come across it when she was online. I knew that she already felt sad that she had been the cause of all the things that had happened to us. So this time I just told her about anything I could think of that was good. And I checked on her health and the kids' activities, including Chiara's interest in books and Ryan's latest progress with vocabulary. I missed them so. We talked about getting Skype when they were sure they'd be staying on the farm.

This caused Jenny to think again about how the house on the property might not be a permanent and secure solution and that something else might have to be organised eventually.

After saying hello to the kids in turn and telling them how much I loved them, I finished the call.

I was determined to avoid the blog, knowing it would only depress me. But I couldn't always obey myself. I was drawn to it. I looked to see what was posted there today. Once again it showed Mac and me in compromising positions with text underneath which was coarse and indecent. I was sorry I'd looked, and fell to weeping quietly on the bed.

Mac arrived home from bowls and found me like this.

'Been looking at the trolling again?' he inquired. 'I told you. Don't look. It doesn't help and it just feeds into John's hands.'

He held me close and eventually I stopped and got up to make a cup of tea. Mac stayed on the bed, happy to have a brief post-bowls nap.

With the harassment and the stalking I'd been feeling daily fear and anger. Now I felt that we had no control over our lives. It was the most horrible feeling I'd ever had. Now I simply couldn't contain my fear and anger.

I saw that the situation had grown out of John's need for dominance, revenge and his wish to isolate his family from the rest of society. He had ruined Jenny's family life. He was ruining the lives of his children through his need to keep them away from our family. He'd caused Mac's blood pressure to spike which could even prove to be a factor in causing death. In all, he'd ruined our finances and my peace of mind forever.

I was so angry I was shaking. My fingers were quivering all on their own. Then the tension moved to my body and I began to shake all over. Blood rushed to my head and my face felt raw. My brain was filled with a hatred I had never felt before, and never wanted to again.

My eyes started to water and my tongue became dry. I couldn't swallow; nor could I breathe easily. My rasping breath was pulled through my mouth in gulps and I could hardly stand. I staggered over to the lounge and collapsed into a soft cushion.

It took all my willpower to calm my breathing. 'Slow down, slow down,' I kept saying to myself like a mantra. After a few minutes my breathing eased and I was able to run my tongue around my mouth, gathering enough saliva so that I could swallow. My body bent inwards to the lounge and started to curl into a ball, and my hands, which had become clenched, unfurled along the lounge chair's arm like two dead fish.

It was a shocking state to be in. I had never felt so helpless and afraid that I would die.

I needed to be the one to remain calm and sensible for Mac. Because he was the one who had high blood pressure which carried a real possibility of a heart attack.

Weeping quietly, I realised my tears had run down my nose to my lips and then dripped onto my lap. So I took myself in hand.

I was resolved to be strong and find a solution to this problem. I would not let John win.

Chapter 23

Jenny was firmly settled into life on the farm well before Christmas.

Mac and I bought more Christmas presents for the kids online as the kids' highlight of the year approached. Finally we realised it was better to have them delivered directly to Jed's property rather than for us to post them. That way John wouldn't know we'd bought anything and therefore wouldn't know where the children were.

But before Christmas celebrations rolled around, Mac and I had our own celebration to enjoy: the weekend of the Scottish Highland Gathering at Bundanoon, near Canberra. Every year about three thousand people descend on Bundanoon, which is called Brigadoon for the day, named after a movie starring Gene Kelly and Van Johnson. There are Scottish bands, typical food, including haggis, clan tents and plenty of fun.

This particular year we were in dire need of cheering up, and wanted to feel proud of our Scottish surname, McGregor, that had been so sullied by John's disgusting trolling. We stayed at a hotel in Mittagong for the weekend which allowed us to stroll around Bowral in the day. It was when we returned home that things went wrong.

The first phone call was just a hang up. We thought nothing about it. How many of these sorts of calls does everyone get each week? Lots. Sometimes we believed that the callers were scammers. They were people who were pretending to be representatives of the bank, Microsoft, Telstra or from Nigeria or the like. We always ignored them by hanging up the phone, or if there were emails, deleting them immediately.

But after several hang-up calls all in one day, we became suspicious.

We put on the answering machine so that all calls could be filtered, and we alerted Jenny, and Tony and Samantha, to explain how to reach us. Our new procedure meant that we wouldn't answer straight away but would wait for the machine to kick in, hear who was leaving a message and then call them back or pick up the phone before the message was finished. It was a bit cumbersome but seemed safer. Most often the callers remained silent, so we were sure it was John who was still proving a pest.

Then one call was different. An unknown voice said, 'Watch out!' That was all. Just, 'Watch out!' Mac and I listened to it a few times, trying to determine the voice, but it was low and guttural and sounded foreign. We gave up.

Over the next week there were more calls. They were getting more explicit every time. Now the voice was saying, 'I will get you', or 'I'm watching every move you make and I will grab you when the time is right.' It was the fifth call in two days, with a message that sounded even more threatening, that made us finally call the police.

Once again, the same two officers, Sgt Ronson and Constable Bailey, came to the door. We played back the messages that were recorded on the machine. Sgt Ronson asked us about enemies again, took notes, and offered us some advice.

'It could be just kids making nuisance calls and they'll soon give up. If it keeps up, we can monitor your calls at the station. It means putting a phone tap on your phone line. Let's see what happens first.'

Mac took a breath, 'We think it's John, our son-in-law, again. All these threats are from him. The blog and the calls. What can you do about it? It's actually affecting our health and sanity.'

The two police officers looked at each other before Sgt Ronson explained the legal facts.

'There's no proof of it being your son-in-law either with the trolling or the phone calls. So there's nothing much we can do without proof. But we'll write a report and make sure all our officers are alerted.'

We could see they could take no action unless something happened where there would be proof.

Mac felt chastened and resigned to the harassment. We said goodbye and Mac saw them to the door.

We both thought John was to blame. His revenge was escalating and we knew instinctively that it wouldn't stop. I looked at Mac. He seemed very pale and not his usual self. I held my hand to his forehead. He was hot.

'Have you taken your blood pressure pills today?' I asked.

'No. With all that was going on, I forgot.'

'Take them now'.

It seemed to me that Mac was looking weaker and frailer than he had last week. I hoped that his health could stand up to this situation. I knew how I felt. I recalled the panic attack I'd experienced the previous week. I also felt afraid a lot of the time, and when I was not afraid I was angry. Both these emotions were not good for my health. They affected me in many ways. Sometimes I woke up with headaches or back aches. Sometimes I was forgetful and did the same job twice. I had caught colds several times in the past few months, a thing I knew happened when I was not feeling positive, happy and on top of things. It was almost as if my state of mind allowed germs to strike.

We went out for a walk. Mac was better out in the sunshine away from the house.

Four doors down, our neighbour came out of his house and walked to his front fence to speak with us. He was a shy man, about 80 years old, with white receding hair, well-worn clothes and had tartan slippers on his shuffling feet. He was obviously wanting to tell us something but didn't have the courage to begin. I thought it was probably about the blog, so I decided to bring it up myself and save him the embarrassment.

'I guess you saw the blog that has been written about us, Dennis?'

He cleared his throat and said in a wavering voice, 'Yeah, I did. And I thought I might have a solution for you.'

'Oh? What is it?'

'My grandson is very good with computers. In fact he's living here with me because my son and daughter-in-law have had enough of him. He was caught hacking into police files to see what he could find. They have given him a warning because he's only fourteen, but one more stunt like that and he'll be charged. I've been trying to keep him busy and away from the computer but that isn't really working. Sometimes when I wake in the night to go to the toilet, I can see under his bedroom door that the light is on. He's a good kid really, but I can't stop him getting to the computer. I thought he could look at your blog and try to find out who's writing it. It would keep him busy with something that is about computers, but isn't illegal. It could help.

I stared at him. How could a fourteen-year-old do more than the police? And then I thought about how he had got into police files that must have been very secure.

'I'd like that,' I said. 'The police have looked at it but haven't discovered anything yet, so someone with a creative mind just might crack it.'

'Thanks,' Dennis said. 'I'm really at a loss to keep him occupied and I never know what he's doing on the computer.'

We walked with Dennis to his front door and then into his foyer so he could call up the stairs from there to his nephew. The boy came slowly down the stairs, scuffling his feet and chewing gum. He was a tall, skinny guy with the start of a teenage moustache, dressed in typical teen clothing of torn jeans, a torn T-shirt and sneakers with holes.

'This is Richard. I asked him before I spoke to you if he could help and he seems to think he can.'

'Hello, Richard,' I said, and Mac nodded a greeting.

Richard grunted and looked at the ground. He blew a bubble of gum and let it snap.

'Would you like to come along to our place now and try or would you like to come another time?' I didn't know if he needed to use our computer to solve our problems, but figured it might be helpful for him to check it anyway.

He slouched against the balustrade with his eyes down and his

Adams-apple bobbing up and down as he answered.

'Okay. Now would be good,' he said in a squeaky voice.

Mac and I turned around and walked back to the house, trailed by Richard. We showed him the computer and answered a few questions, giving him the passwords and programmes we used. Then we left him to it. I peeked back at him as we went out onto the verandah at the back of the house. He looked different somehow. His face had come alive and he sat up straight. He looked confident. It was amazing to me how a person could change when they found something that they liked to do.

Mac and I stayed in and around the house for the rest of the afternoon. Every now and then I peeked into the lounge room to offer Richard a drink or a biscuit. He took everything offered but didn't stop banging on the keyboard. By late afternoon he came out to find us. He seemed deflated and ashamed to tell us that he couldn't find the source of the blog.

'Never mind,' I said. 'The police haven't had any luck either.'

'I thought I'd found it when I went into your emails,' he said. 'But it was someone who has been hacking into them. Maybe you'd like to see.'

Mac and I gazed at the computer screen. 'Look here,' said Richard. 'Since October someone has been reading your emails.'

Mac and I looked at the screen. We couldn't understand what Richard was showing us, but we believed him. The timing was right. That was after we'd spirited Jenny away. It was sure to have been John.

'Can you stop the person looking at our emails?'

'Sure,' said Richard. 'I'll just get some more security for you as well as putting a block on anyone who tries to see them.'

He looked pleased that he'd been able to do something to help us, even if he couldn't find out who was writing the blog. Mac and I thanked him, Mac shaking his hand in a manly way. Richard perked up about this. I felt that most people treated him like a naughty little kid, which of course he was, but we realised he was also knowledgeable and close to being a man.

I wondered if the police would find this hacker as Richard had done. Maybe their search was too confined to the blog. I'd been puzzled about how John had known where we were when the blue Mazda was spying on us at the shops or a friend's house. We had also wondered how he knew when we were not at home, so that he could destroy something at the house. Now we knew. Mac and I mainly emailed friends to say we were coming to an event. And I would also send Tony information about what we were going to do and where we'd be, as he liked to keep tabs on our movements. I guess he thought we were 'old codgers', a term he'd first used when he was a teenager.

Mac and I conferred on what sort of things we'd written in our emails. Thank goodness we'd decided never to reveal Jenny's situation or email her.

She was still safe.

Chapter 24

Jed sat on his tractor and watched Jenny and the kids trudge up from the manager's house to his home. Both children were scampering here and there, picking up stones and throwing them at the trees. They seemed very happy.

His heart flipped as he looked at Jenny. He'd really fallen for her. She was such a petite little thing but with a strong core of confidence about protecting her children that had been strengthening every day since she'd left Sydney, he thought.

Jed had never married. He'd never found the right woman, one who was prepared to share the workload of a farm with him. Several women from the local town had been friends and that bond probably could have become more than that, but Jed had been busy making his business grow at the time, travelling a lot in order to expand his markets.

He'd been sent to boarding school from age nine to eighteen, only coming home on school holidays. At first he'd missed his mother terribly, and Melbourne had been a frightening place away from family and everything familiar, but by the time of his adolescence he'd made firm friends for life, and he was used to city life and rather liked it. At home every holiday, he helped on the farm, 'learning the ropes' from his dad. During his childhood, the farm was mainly for sheep, with a few cattle and a stand of fruit trees. But in the 1950s the sheep industry flagged.

With the advent of synthetic materials, wool wasn't as popular as it had been, and lamb was cheap.

By the time Jed left school for university to learn about animal husbandry, he'd become interested in expanding the farm to focus on vealers and reducing the stock of sheep. By this stage his dad was eighty and, understandably, not inclined to work as hard as he had done all his life. He and Jed's mother wanted to sit on the porch, view their property and see it prosper. His father was glad that Jed had shown an interest in maintaining the farm. He'd feared that Jed would find the lure of the city too great and leave him with a property that would have to be sold. His parents were so relieved Jed was returning home they deeded the farm, along with some funds for improvement, to Jed on his 21st birthday, and then moved into town.

At first Jed found that helping on a farm and running the farm were two different things. The skills he'd learned with his dad and at university came in handy but there was nothing like being there every day and finding ways to maximise his business by working with others. Eventually he'd started making a profit and was now quite well off, even through the bad years of drought and bushfire. It was time to think about a family to carry on his efforts.

He'd been attracted to Jenny on first sighting in Sydney over the wall of the house next door. But it had been during this time in Victoria spent with her at home that had convinced him that he would take their romantic beginnings further. She'd shown such a strong spirit in leaving her old life and creating a new one for the children and herself. She was also a hard worker, interested in everything that was happening around her, a great mum, kind and generous, and had a sense of humour that matched his. He wondered whether she would be happy on a farm the size of his, and be content to live there forever.

He frowned as he thought about her husband, John. It was obvious he wasn't happy to let her go and might cause trouble.

Well, Jed thought, if he couldn't marry her, he would just live with her. His thoughts of marriage came as a shock to him. He'd been thinking of her staying on the farm but he hadn't thought of marriage. Now he was. Yes, that was what he wanted – marriage, a home and a family.

More kids that would be his and Jenny's. Kids that could grow to work beside him on the farm. Of course, he would never neglect Jenny's children, he thought, but it would be nice to have a son or daughter of his own. He knew that his mother and father had despaired of him marrying to keep the family name going. They would have loved Jenny he thought, especially his mum, as she'd had the same spirit that Jenny showed.

Jed fired up the tractor, and as Jenny heard the noise and waved Jed waved back. This is what he wanted and, he realised now, what he'd wanted for a long time. There'd been a hole in his life that could now be filled, if Jenny was inclined to say yes.

If this John character came around, Jed would be ready to tell him where to get off and what to do with his life. He would fight for her and the kids as long as he had breath in his body.

Jed felt he needed to see Jenny right then. He hadn't thought much about marriage before now, and found he needed to just be close to her.

'Come and meet the new pups,' he called to Chiara and

Ryan as his housekeeper, Tamara, came out of the laundry where they were being kept warm.

Chiara and Ryan bounced across the concrete to the laundry door. Jenny could hear Tamara telling them which was a girl and which was a boy, and asking them what names they would call them.

Jed looked at Jenny. 'That will keep them busy for a while.' His passionate glance locked onto hers. Then his warm hand clasped hers, and he pulled her towards him until their bodies touched. She relaxed into his arms, pressing her cheek to his chest.

'I think I need you beside me,' Jed murmured. 'You give me such comfort and pleasure. You make me feel complete.'

Jenny looked up at his thoughtful face. He was so dear to her. Her arms reached up around his shoulders and she held him still, looking deeply into his eyes.

'I feel the same way,' she said softly. 'I want to stay in your arms forever.'

Gently he bent his head toward her and rubbed his lips softly against hers, then deepened this into a kiss that held all the longing he felt, and took Jenny's breath away.

'Mummy, come and see the puppies,' Ryan yelled, waving his arms in the air from the doorway of the laundry. 'The one I love is so cute.'

Jenny pulled away from Jed, still holding his hand.

'Mine's cute too,' she whispered, still looking at Jed, before she hurried off to see Ryan and his puppy.

Chapter 25

When Tony and Samantha asked if we'd like to visit them in Brisbane for Christmas, I jumped at the chance.

Mac and I decided we'd fly up there rather than drive. Qantas was offering cheap flights for Christmas so I went onto the website and, using our frequent flyer points, booked two return flights for a week.

It was the first time we'd seen their new home. Samantha had been very upset by all the things that had been happening to us in Sydney, and as they'd been considering moving for some time, they decided to go back to Brisbane where her family lived. And we could see what a bargain Brisbane housing was. Their home was on a headland above a small beach on Morton Bay, just out of Brisbane city. The breeze drifted in over the bay, keeping the house cool even though, like all Queenslanders, they had ducted aircon.

'It's just the house to raise a family in,' Samantha said, with a twinkle in her eyes.

'Does this mean …?' I trailed off, trying to read her look.

'Yes,' said Tony. 'You're the first to know. The baby is due in July next year.'

After lots of hugs, congratulations and champagne which Tony, Mac and I drank, but Samantha declined, we started to talk about baby rooms, cots, strollers, car seats and clothes they would need. Tony and

Mac rolled their eyes and decided to go for a walk.

Christmas Day was wonderful, with a tree that we all took part in decorating, an alfresco dinner of seafood and Christmas pudding, and lots of presents. I'd gone shopping in Brisbane the day after I heard the news of the baby, to buy the first of many nighties, singlets and bibs.

We were also able to Skype Jenny and the kids at Jed's house. It had been months since we'd seen the children and I regretted this when we all noted how they'd grown and changed. Jenny was very excited to hear the news about the baby. I could see, though, that she was holding back tears, I guess because she was thinking how much she'd like to be with us all. She might even have thought she'd never see Tony and Samantha again in the flesh, or the baby to come.

Just a few days later we were on the plane back home again. Mac and I were so buoyed up that the issues of what might have happened at our house while we were away didn't occur to us until we turned into our street. Thank God it was still safe and sound, I thought.

I gazed at the house. The neighbours had agreed to keep an eye on it, which was undoubtedly more effective than the irregular police patrols. Jean was also collecting our mail and when she saw the taxi pull up, she bounded over the road with a pile of letters.

We invited her in for a cup of tea, but she could see we were tired and said she would catch up later.

We sat in the kitchen and began opening the mail. There were a few Christmas cards that had not reached us before the day, and a pile of official looking envelopes. Mac tore the first one open and gasped in horror. He passed it across to me and I read it slowly, trying to take it all in. There were just two paragraphs typed in the middle of the page. They read:

Beware and be afraid. Those who treat others in the wrong way will be avenged.

At once all the happy thoughts and memories of Christmas fled from my mind. It was starting again, only in a new form this time, I guess because John had had trouble hacking into our emails since Richard had put a block on our account. I grabbed a few more of the letters in similar envelopes and tore them open. They all had the same two paragraphs and the same words on them.

There were six messages in all.

Once again we called the police who came around to our house, smartly this time. We explained that we had been away and showed them what was waiting for us on our return. They looked at the letters and remarked on the commonness of the paper, the print, the envelopes, the stamps and the printed address.

They told us there was no point in having the stamps DNA tested for saliva from licking because they were all current stamps with self-sticking backs. We though that this was the case. Everybody knew about DNA from CSI.

The police prodded us with the same questions as before, such as, 'Do you know who might have done it?', 'Has there been some issue that would cause people to write this to you?', 'Do you have any enemies?' And lastly, 'Could this be related to the harassment you had been experiencing earlier in the year with the trolling?'

We nodded, feeling helpless.

After they'd left I said to Mac, 'Why don't we just tell them more about John without disclosing anything about Jenny? We could just say that his mother in England said he is a rather vengeful person and he could be taking his revenge this way.'

Mac's response was as cautious as it was wise.

'I'm worried that if we say anything about Jenny leaving him they might want to talk to her. What would we do? I don't want to give her location away as John might discover it. Besides, Jenny has asked us not to tell anyone.'

I sighed. I seemed to be sighing so often these last six months. We were stuck.

At least there'd been no more destruction of our property. This letter writing seemed to have replaced it – and we didn't know it then but it would continue for some time. We received a new letter every two days or so. We kept them all to show the police, but began to recognise them from the envelopes and, rather than open them, just put them in a box for collection.

Mac went back to bowls and I re-enrolled in ukulele, creative writing and watercolour painting classes online for the following year, even though classes wouldn't start until the new school term began at the end of January.

New Year's Eve was the next day. We were concerned that John would plan something terrible for us. We decided to stay home rather than go down to the Motor Yacht Club on Pittwater and watch the fireworks.

Once again John was controlling our lives.

Chapter 26

The blog had been the cause of a wave of anger against us. There had been over 30,000 hits on the site as stated by the site counter and people had responded in the comments section.

Anyone could make a comment about what they'd read or seen, and post it there for all to read and also to respond to. People who commented were never clearly identified because most had a nickname or just used a first name.

I read a few of the posts and found that most were absolutely nasty comments as readers believed what was being written about us.

The posts ranged from, 'I cannot believe anyone can be so stupid. They mustn't have a brain in their heads' to 'I'm horrified about the sickening things these two people do. They should be shot.'

I wanted to write my own message and say it was all made up but of course I didn't dare. I couldn't be like them. I wasn't even able to defend myself.

Mac and I talked about John. How could he be like this?

On a whim one day while I was on the computer, I googled 'revenge'. About 100 sites came up all relating to revenge. A few tried to explain revenge, saying it was the smart way to behave because although vengeance was evil, it was, 'Oh, so sweet'.

One or two sites advised that even though we might be victims, we needed to accept our fate. This didn't sound right to me. I kept on looking at the sites and was concerned to discover that most of them were offering ways to get revenge.

One site had a list of ways they could provide revenge on anyone, ranging from nuisance calls to the person one wanted to take vengeance on, twisted gifts, or nasty bumper stickers on cars. Scammers advertised that they could scam money, send abusive emails or post nasty cards to the person of your choice, or even set up a blog about them. In each case they posed questions such as, 'Is your boss horrible to you? Do your parents treat you badly? Are you sick of your neighbours?'

I was appalled.

How could people think they were getting justice by causing more harm than good? One site offered information on people who were vengeful. I clicked on it.

This site talked about how these people had a need to be needed and when they weren't needed they became resentful. These people were often obsessive/compulsive in their thinking and couldn't focus on daily activities, as their minds were filled with the petty revenge they wanted to inflict and in blaming others.

I thought about John and realised that he had some of these characteristics. We had not known it and neither had Jenny because, the article revealed, these people often used charm to get what they wanted. It was only after experiencing something like this that I could see the charm had been fake and had had a purpose, to ultimately completely control Jenny and the children.

The site said that these people often had low self-esteem and were usually controlling, or sometimes in a co-dependency relationship or no relationship at all as they found it difficult to form intimate relationships. Add to this a violent temper and they could abuse others or seek revenge, sometimes for years.

Years! How could we stand this for years?

There were no sites that told us what we could do to get rid of the person seeking revenge.

Mac and I hadn't realised that revenge was such a common occurrence. Mac remembered a neighbour who hadn't liked the fellow across the road parking in front of his house, so had placed flies on a piece of rotten meat in the boot, so that the heat in the boot would cause the flies to breed and cause trouble when he opened it after he came home from an overseas trip.

I also remembered a worker in an office who had wanted revenge on her boss. She had made a complaint about sexual harassment that could not be proven, but had ruined this person's chances of advancement.

Of course this led to us thinking of times gone by when the Corleones took revenge on anyone they thought was doing the wrong thing by them; and the whole history of war in Middle East seemed to be built on revenge over territory that had been going on for centuries.

When we talked about this, we realised that revenge had possibly started with early humans and was still in force today. As if it was built into our consciousness or instinctive. This didn't feel very encouraging.

I wondered if the best thing to do was to try again to talk to John. This was always what we advocated when we talked about the futility of going to war in Iraq or Afghanistan.

'I wish they would get together and talk through their issues instead of just starting a war,' was what we would say.

But how could we find John? We looked up the online directory for residents' phone numbers and also the reverse directory. Either he had a mobile that was blocked or no landline phone.

I thought Jenny might know a friend of John's who could advise us where he was now. So I rang her. Jenny was horrified.

'You want to talk to him? I know what will happen. He'll use his charm to get information out of you to figure out where I am and will take even more opportunities to harass you. Please don't do it. Please, Mum.'

What could I do but obey my daughter's wishes?

Chapter 27

That afternoon Jenny took the children to the library.

A small brick building in the centre of town, it was also used as the local community centre and meeting room. She thought the library might be a little old fashioned as country libraries sometimes missed out on the newest books for children. But this wasn't the case.

There was a sunny corner with views of the paddocks nearby. The corner had shelves that displayed children's books so they could see the covers and could easily reach them.

There were small chairs and tables for those who wanted to sit and also comfy lounges for mothers and children who wanted to read while they were there.

Jenny took a book she knew to be their favourite over to the lounges and they settled in to hear the story. She thought back to her teaching job. *I've missed all this. Reading to the children was one of my most treasured jobs.*

She started to read and began playing all the characters in the book with their accents and drama. Soon a few other children sidled up to where they were and in no time she had a group of five children, rapt, all listening to the story.

Jenny was having such fun that she couldn't stop. She read several more books that Ryan, Chiara and some other children picked out, giving

the stories her dramatic interpretation. In some she even added appropri-
ate songs and action rhymes. When it was over the children went reluctantly back to their mums and dads.

The librarian came over to Jenny.

'That was magnificent. We haven't had a story corner for a long
time. I'm too busy to do it anymore. Would you care to come in once a
week for a couple of hours and read or tell stories? I can't pay you as
there are no funds available but if you're interested I could advertise it
in the newsletter and put a note on the board so that parents could come.'

Jenny thought about it. It was not a paid job but she didn't think
she would be able to find a paid job at present anyway, and this was what
she really liked to do. It also meant that Ryan and Chiara would get to
know some of the children from the town.

Jenny said yes and took Chiara and Ryan home to think up some
ideas to amuse the children in story time. All three of them hurried up to
Jed's house to tell him the good news.

'I don't think anyone will find me at the library, especially in the
story corner,' Jenny said.

Jed scooted out from under the tractor on his low platform. He sat
up and looked at Jenny.

'Very nice! I might even come round to the library to listen as
well.' He winked at Chiara and Ryan. They giggled.

'You're too big,' said Ryan giving Jed a soft punch on the arm.

Jenny watched Ryan and Jed spar for a minute and thought how
well they were accepting him, and how much he seemed to like them.

Jenny's new unpaid job took hold over the school holidays. Chiara liked helping Jenny give out papers to colour in, designed around the stories she was reading, and Ryan liked packing up the books after the session was over. They both enjoyed a little special reading time with Jenny after everyone had gone.

Soon there were more than forty children and parents at story corner. Jenny asked if she could split the event into two sessions so the children could get the best out of the program.

The librarian agreed and so the one story time turned out to be two sessions on one day and another session on the next day. The children began turning up in fairy costumes and pirate hats. The parents became as enthusiastic as the children and soon teddies came on days when a teddy bear story was programmed and wands arrived when there was to be a story about magic.

Jenny thought Jed would be tired of her talking about the sessions, but he seemed to like to hear about them. He even found old books that he'd had as a child and bits and pieces that matched the story of the day such as a toy dog for Jez Alborough's Some Dogs Do stories. Everything seemed to be peaceful and Jenny began to relax.

Most evenings Jenny and the kids would trundle up to Jed's house for a swim and Jed would often come down to their house for dinner.

Jenny would get tingles up her spine when Jed was near. How hard had she fallen for him? How disloyal was she? She'd only been separated from John for six months even though she'd come to distrust and dislike him long before that.

One evening they walked down to Jenny's house for dinner, with the kids running ahead and climbing the fence rails in the alley between the paddocks. It was a very good thing Jed had never had these fences electrified, Jenny thought. Jed took Jenny's hand.

'You know, I've never felt so at home with anyone. I love being with you.'

'I feel that way too,' she whispered.

Jed pulled her to him, gave her a soft quick kiss and said, 'That's just a taster. We'll find time for the real meal when the kids are in bed.'

………………..

Jenny sat on the side of Chiara's bed. Ryan was already asleep, his body twisted around so that his head was towards the end of the bed and his feet on the pillow. The sheet lay half on the floor along with his teddy.

'When is Daddy coming home?' her voice piped up.

Jenny gulped. How do I answer this? What is best? A lie, the truth, or a mixture?

'Daddy's in Sydney.'

'Where is he staying? Why doesn't he come to Victoria where we are?'

'He's busy, sweetheart. He's got things to do in Sydney.'

'Doesn't he love us anymore?'

'Of course he loves you. He'll never stop loving you. That will never happen.'

'Do you still love Daddy?'

Jenny gazed at Chiara. This was the time to say something of the situation.

'Mummies and Daddies sometimes don't love each other any-more. I think your daddy and I don't love each other the same as before.'

'Will you get a divorce? Marcie at the Library is divorced. Marcie has a new boyfriend. He's nice. Marcie might marry him. Would you like a divorce too, Mummy?'

'I don't know yet, sweetheart. Maybe. Sometime. But not now. I'm too busy looking after you and Ryan and reading to the children in the library.'

She gave Chiara a little tickle. 'Although. I do have my assistant to help me.'

Chiara giggled. 'You mean me, don't you, Mummy?'

'I do. You're the best helper in the world.'

'Maybe I'll be a librarian when I grow up.'

Jenny gave her a big kiss and covered her with the sheet. 'Go to sleep now, Chiara. See you later, Alligator.'

'In a while Crocodile,' a sleepy Chiara responded.

As Jenny partly shut the bedroom door behind her, making sure there was a little light streaming into the room, she thought about John and Jed, how different they were, and how she had some residue of feeling for John that still caused her to feel guilt sometimes.

Perhaps she needed to finish with John before taking an interest in Jed. But how? She didn't want John to know where she was. So how could she get a divorce? She sighed. Nothing was simple.

She was in the kitchen, pouring herself a glass of wine before going back to Jed in the lounge room, when he appeared at the door. *Almost as if I called him to help, she thought.*

'Hi,' he said softly, slowly coming into the kitchen.

'Hi, yourself,' Jenny answered. She held up the bottle with a question in her eyes.

'No, I'll have a beer.'

Jenny went to the fridge and opened it. Jed strode swiftly up behind her, putting his arms around her waist and pulling her to his chest. He groaned as he moved his hands up to her breasts.

'You feel so soft and warm. I want you Jenny.'

Jenny was suddenly conflicted. One minute she had been with Chiara, talking about John, love and divorce. The next minute she was in Jed's arms.

She pushed herself away from him as she slammed the fridge door.

'I can't do this. It isn't right. I'm married and have two children who love their dad. Besides who'd want a person who was so weak that she let her husband dominate her for years?'

Jenny stood against the kitchen table breathing heavily, shaking. Jed took one step towards her and folded her in his arms.

'You're the most wonderful woman I've ever known. Smart, sensible, creative, and a loving mother. Everything you used to put up with was for the children. But John isn't here now and never will be as long as I have something to say about it. So stop worrying, and start letting the love you hold inside you come out, and love me instead.'

Suddenly the tension dissipated and Jenny slumped in his arms. She looked tearfully up at Jed. His strong jaw. His kind eyes. His thick hair. The love she had kept partly hidden inside her burst open and she reached up to touch his face and pull his head toward her for her kiss. A kiss that was deep and open and clearly said, 'I love you'.

In a moment he'd walked her backwards to the sofa, where he gently laid her down, following her with his strong body.

Tenderly, he held her face so she couldn't escape his eyes. Jenny caught her breath in wonder.

'I'm in love with you,' Jed murmured. 'You give me happiness. You give me peace.' He smiled down at her. 'You give me lustful ideas.'

He touched her lips which were soft and warm and wet with anticipation. Then he deepened his hold on her, leaning his chin toward her mouth to meet her lips in a sizzling kiss that held her in thrall.

His hands swept down her body, warm and sure, caressing each part of her as he did so. Her mind spun into free fall with the love and gentleness of it. Then his caresses became firmer and stronger with a need that could not be answered with kisses alone.

Jenny arched up towards him trying to capture his body in hers, as she pulled off her jeans and top. This was what she wanted. Someone she loved and who loved her with no reserves. Someone she could hold in her heart forever while trusting that he would feel the same. She pressed herself to his body and let her mind immerse herself in an intensity of love.

....

The story telling corner was a great hit. Soon the librarian asked Jenny if she would like to go out with the mobile library van, which delivered books to remote areas, and give them a story time. Jenny of course said yes, as long as she could take Ryan and Chiara with her. This was agreed and Jenny found herself getting to know the country communities of Apollo Bay, Port Fairy, Dimboola, Keith and Rainbow Lake.

Usually the van parked near the town community centre or the local park. The days had been announced in a calendar of events for the community, and people came from up to 100 kilometres away to participate.

Jenny was told that during term the children attending would mostly be pre-schoolers, but during school holidays there was always a rush with older kids coming in, and Jenny found that she was catering for 5 to 12-year-olds who were all thirsting for stories and fun.

Jenny began to include drama and puppetry as well as singing and action into story time. She also became quite close to some of the regular children who mostly studied through School of the Air during term time and relished the chance to meet face-to-face with a teacher.

The parents also enjoyed the sessions because they gave them a chance to relax, unlike School of the Air, which required their presence to oversee the students' work, so as well as their farm work, the parents' days were always busy and tiring.

Jenny felt that she had made a new career for herself here. One that the kids enjoyed too. And she looked forward to a strong enduring relationship with Jed into the future.

When Jenny thought about the future, she didn't know how it would end up. How could she divorce John? If he found her, there might be more trouble. She needed to think of the children first, not her own needs.

But for the first time in years, Jenny was able to relax. Her thoughts were now imbued with confidence. There was no way John would be able to find her out there, she decided.

Chapter 28

Now, two weeks had passed since anything much had happened to Mac or me.

The week before had been Australia Day. We usually went by ferry into the Botanic Gardens to see the fireworks. Mac firmly believed we should go again this year to buck up our spirits, so we went early, trailing our chairs and picnic hamper to the spot where we usually sat, giving us a good view of the Harbour Bridge.

The Opera House had been lit up with Aboriginal designs across its famous sails. Small yachts and other boats bobbed up and down near the bridge, jockeying for best viewing position near the pontoons that housed some of the fireworks.

The smallest fireworks sparks started near the closest pylon and fizzed across the arch of the bridge before bursting into curls and flowers above it, popping and sparkling in the night sky. The final spectacle was a stream of white lights sprinting across the straight section of the bridge, until it plummeted into a waterfall of brilliant white sparkles that rained down into the water. Every one gave a loud cheer as this occurred. It was a feature that we later thought was better than all the fireworks in London and New York.

Mac and I turned to each other and said the right words, 'How wonderful, better than last year.' But our hearts weren't in it. Most of the magic and excitement of it all had been stolen from us and replaced with a grey foggy cloud. One that I could almost see out of the corner of my eye. But when I turned to look, it would be gone. It seemed chokingly tangible and was stalking me. It was fear.

I was still angry that John was spoiling our lives.

At home the next day we wondered if he would become tired of this. I mentioned to Mac that I had read that revengeful people could carry on like this for years. He would feel the need to be skirting around us in his Mazda, following us regularly. But how would this interfere with his job, whatever that was now?

We knew that he was quite a clever person with great IT skills, and probably found it easy to find new jobs. Many IT jobs could also be found where one could work from home, so that might be why he could follow us so easily.

Full summer was upon us. New fashions were in the shops, and I wanted to explore and buy something to cheer myself up. Mac had smiled at me and said a new dress would surely buck me up. I thought so too.

Warringah Mall seemed to be the best place to go, with two major shops, Myers and David Jones, plus a number of little speciality shops. So I took myself off one afternoon and had a great time browsing and trying on clothes. I also couldn't help looking in the book section for books for the grandchildren, even though I was wary of being seen to buy any, in case John was watching. Mac and I had learned to be careful about showing any interest in the children as it could indicate that we knew where Jenny and the children were.

I was so caught up in the enjoyment and freedom of my shopping spree that it was past 5.30 when I realised the time. I quickly rushed to the underground carpark. Although daylight saving had put our clocks forward one hour, inside the carpark it looked dark.

There were a small number of cars lined up at the card exit gate. That left only a few cars in the carpark itself. They were scattered around the place on each of the floors with vast empty sections in between. I had parked on the middle floor to be close to the David Jones entry where I thought I might find something nice to wear. Mine was the only car at that level and the carpark looked empty and quiet.

Suddenly I became frightened. I told myself not to be silly. I had experienced that feeling of someone behind me on many occasions and discovered there was no-one there. But I had also seen many movies where there was someone following a woman who would later be murdered. I couldn't stop my body's reaction to the loneliness and echoing quietness. I knew that this was just preservation-thinking. It was a good thing to be aware of who or what was around you so that you could be on guard. But because of all the strange things that had been happening to us, I was doubly scared.

I stood stock still and looked around.

In the far corner of the floor there was a mother putting children into her car and buckling them in. If someone was after me she would be too far away to help. As I watched, she pulled out and drove down the ramp to the exit.

There was no one near me now and my car was quite a distance from the lift I had taken down from David Jones. Shaking myself and calling myself all sorts of names, I fumbled in my purse for the car keys. I had picked up the second set of keys that had no remote attachment. You actually had to put the key in the lock and turn it.

I held the key in my hand like a knife with the pointed end through my fingers. I purposefully strode over to the car, keeping a watch left and right.

As I reached my hand to the key slot in the driver's door I was grabbed from behind. My scream was cut off into a gargle by a hand covering and sinking into my mouth, and a strong male body crushed me against the side of the door with the key and handle biting into my middle. For a moment I was so scared that I couldn't resist. Then anger overcame me. What was I doing letting a villain grab me. I'd been to self-defence lessons and talks on what to do if you are assaulted. I had to fight back.

My anger sustained me and gave me more strength than I would normally have had. I lashed out with my other hand which had been resting on the side of the car, coming full circle around so that my elbow crashed into the man's shoulder. In the process my body was wrenched sideways as he had now had me tight in his grip, facing the car. But it was just that surprise act that made him move to avoid the hit on his shoulder, which lightened his crushing hold on me.

Now screaming loudly, I continued to swing around, so that I was facing him with my back to the car door. I would not be able to step backwards; in fact I was trapped between the car and the man. The only way to go was forward. I lifted my foot and brought it down with as much force as I could, hoping that it would land on his toes or at least his shin.

He let out a yelp and muffled my scream again with his palm. My right hand was in his grasp and he was grinding the bones together. The pain was excruciating.

I could now see his form clearly. He was short and stocky and wore a crash helmet on his head so I couldn't see his face.

My first surprise blow had been mostly ineffectual, apart from its surprise element. I tried using my shoulders and elbows and head to get some momentum. My knees were free and I brought one up hoping to connect with part of him. He had swung to the side to escape such an action from me but I was still able to hit him in the knee and thigh, although not very forcefully. I reached out, grabbing the arm that was now holding my wrist. His sleeve twisted up and I saw a tattoo of a lion on his wrist.

My strength was spent, his body just crashed into me and I was crushed helpless against the car again. His helmet was against my face and kept it in place against the car. I couldn't move. Thoughts of dying there in the Mall carpark filled my mind. He began to hurl abuse at me now and although I was in pain and terrified I could hear what the words were.

'Get out of his life.' I stood silent and still. *Does he mean John? Is this another threat?* He said it again in a louder voice which was muffled by the helmet. 'Get out of his life.' Then he let go abruptly and ran across the concrete to a motor bike that I hadn't noticed before.

I knew I should rush after him and memorise the number plate of the bike, but instead my body just slid down the car door and I ended up on the cold concrete. I was shaking and gasping big gulps of air, not able to catch my breath properly. Another panic attack. I tried to breathe in and couldn't get enough air. My lips were dry and I couldn't swallow. My legs felt like jelly and there was no way I could get up.

Slowly, I turned over onto my hands and knees and struggled to get up that way, but the muscles in my legs wouldn't work. Swivelling around to the car door, I reached up to grab the handle. From that position I was able then to lever myself up and lean against the door. I was still trying to breathe evenly. The harsh sound of my breathing was so loud that a latecomer looking for his car yelled out from across the space.

'Is something wrong? Can I help?'

I looked at him. He didn't have a helmet, and dressed in a nice suit and tie, he looked harmless. It couldn't be the same person. Even though my breathing still sounded rough, I waved to him and doubled myself over because I couldn't speak. I thought this would be the best way to show I needed help. He rushed to my side and helped me into the car leaving the door open so that he could watch my movements.

Then the man reached for his mobile and asked for an ambulance, looking around to confirm what floor we were on as he spoke to them. Two security guards, having heard the screams also ran into the carpark and rushed to help me.

Their calm voices and steady hands on my back and arms helped me immensely. My breathing began to slow down. Eventually, I began to explain what had happened. They looked around for the motor bike, but I knew it had long gone.

I didn't want to go to hospital. I wanted to go home. 'You've just had a shock,' they said. But as I was a senior I should be in hospital, they told me.

After the paramedics arrived there was some debate about whether I'd go to hospital, but I continued to resist so they treated me there and then let me go home in a taxi. The security guards were most anxious that I wouldn't sue them and asked me to sign a liability form of some kind, took down some information from the passer-by who had helped and then helped me into the taxi they'd called. The last I saw of the scene was my car being locked and left in the carpark alone.

Chapter 29

In dim light, Jenny and Jed were at the computer and she was watching his face in the light from the screen. It was a kind, strong face. A little weather-beaten, but handsome just the same.

He felt the stare and turned to her. 'Don't worry,' he smiled, 'we'll fix it. Just wait and see.'

She couldn't tell him she was really watching him and thinking how wonderful he was. How he made her heart beat faster and her breath catch in her throat. She wasn't sure how he felt. Anyway, she didn't really know how she felt. She got a tingle every time she looked at him. She wanted to be with him and sought him out at every opportunity. But was this real affection, or just thankfulness for someone who was willing to help her? Or even just lust?

She didn't know and couldn't quite trust the strength of her feelings.

Jed had scanned in the birth certificate for his niece. She was born in the same year as Chiara and if Jed could doctor the document, it would make a suitable certificate to show the school principal. First he spread a box shape over his niece's first name. This showed up as a very white box on paper that had a special weave in it.

Jed turned to Jenny. 'I can't copy this original because of the weave in the paper. It's a feature that would show up on the copy. I'll have to do it onto clear white paper so that the weave doesn't mark it. I might have to do it several times until it fades away.'

Jenny waited at the copier and handed him the first sheet as it appeared. Jed then put it back into the scanner and made a new copy of the scanned copy. This time when he printed it, the weave was so faint that he thought it might work.

Once again he spread a box over the first name of his niece, fiddling with the colour wheel as he did so. This time the colour of the box merged with the colour of the page. Great. He sat back with satisfaction.

'This should do it. Now to write in a name for Chiara. It's best to keep something close to her real name as she is likely to forget the new one.'

Jenny thought for a moment. 'You're right. When Mum and Dad had false identities made for the kids, Mum considered the name Keira, although in the end they didn't use it. She felt it would be close enough, that if Chiara forgot her name and said Chiara to anyone, they would think she was playing around with her name. It would also mean that if John was looking for records, he would be looking for a C or CH and not a K.'

Jed looked at the type face for the original surname. It was Heath, his married sister's name.

'Keira Heath sounds pretty good to me,' he said. He typed it in with the same font type and printed it out. They looked carefully at the copy.

'It looks pretty good to me,' said Jenny.

'I think so too,' said Jed. They smiled at each other.

'As long as they don't ask for an original, we'll be safe.'

Jenny was so elated she swung her arms around Jed's neck and gave him a big kiss. Jed responded in kind. Suddenly they separated.

'Sorry,' Jenny murmured. 'I got carried away.'

'I'm glad you did,' said Jed, smiling down at her. 'Let's get carried away some more.'

Jenny smiled at him. 'It sounds like a good idea to me,' she said as she grabbed his hand. 'Only let's get more comfortable.'

She let go of his hand, turned and stepped forward, her back to him, crossing her arms, lifting her T-shirt over her head and dropping it on the floor.

Jed took a breath as his eyes settled on her slightly burnt shoulders with a smattering of freckles, her creamy back tapering to a narrow waist that flared into wider hips in her low rider jeans.

He took the few steps forward to splay his hands on her waist and pull her towards him. She felt his taut body, now divested of his T-shirt, against her back, slightly slick from the heat of the summer day, pressed against hers. He smelled of hay and gun oil and lust. She turned slowly around until her body, soft and cool, melded to his chest.

Skin on skin, heat on heat, they crushed together, settling into the dips and hills of each other's bodies.

Jed slid his arms up her back forcing hers to drape around his neck. He cupped her head and threaded his fingers through her hair, curls bouncing off his fingers, thumbs massaging her softly. He tilted her head up to meet his eyes, clear and blue.

'Do you want this as much as I do?' His voice was hushed.

Mute, Jenny nodded, pulling his head down to meet hers. He took in the softness of her lips, their pinkish-red hue, their tiny grooves ready to be kissed. She licked them tentatively, and he took a deep breath, pushing his lips into the wetness of hers. His hot breath filled her mouth and spread into her throat, filling her being.

Still standing, he curled his body around hers, trying to get even closer, to become one, to be part of her, to love her. Jenny shivered with need, an ache in her stomach, a catch in her heart. He was surrounding her so that every part of her was in touch with him. She could feel his heart thumping in his chest, matched with hers.

In one movement, he lifted her so that she could twist her legs around his waist. He swayed, balancing her weight as he moved towards the open bedroom door. *He's so strong*, Jenny thought.

'Where are the kids?' he asked, his voice gravelly, close to her ear.

'On the tractor in the top paddock, with Jack.'

'Good. I hope they take their time, so that I have plenty of time with you.'

He carried Jenny through the doorway into the bedroom, kicking the door shut behind him with his heel.

………………..

The next day Jenny met the school principal. He was a tall fellow, very stooped, as if he had been marking too many books for too many years at small children's small desks. His eyes though were alert and business-like.

Jenny held out her hand. 'I'm Jenny Sss … Oh … Heath, Keira's mother,' she stammered, remembering at the last minute that if Chiara was Heath then so was she.

'Bill Docker, Principal. What's the 'S …' for?' he asked.

'What?' Jenny looked lost for a minute. 'It's just my middle name, Samantha. I'm so used to saying the whole name for my last job that I forgot you don't need it.'

'Oh, what job was that?' Bill asked casually.

Jenny didn't think he was being nosy, just responding to her statement.

She wracked her brain. 'Just in the media,' she said, hoping that the media would have a section where a middle name would be needed and that Bill Docker wouldn't question her about the job.

He didn't. He held out his hand for the certificate. Jenny had put it in an envelope. She was hoping that it would go on the desk with others and be lost in the paperwork. And this strategy worked. Bill threw it on the desk and it landed in the in-tray with a lot of other envelopes and papers.

Good.

'There's a "Getting to Know your Teacher" session next week,' he said. 'I'd like your daughter to come along. It's one way we have of reducing those first day nerves. This is a small school and most of the kids know each other from the neighbourhood. Keira will be the only one who knows nobody.'

'Thank you, I'm sure she'll like that and I appreciate your concern.' Jenny smiled and with a wave and a nod turned to leave.

'See you next week if I have time. Otherwise I'll see you when school starts.' Bill smiled too and watched her leave. *A nice looking woman that,* he thought.

The next week, before Chiara and Jenny went off to attend the "Getting to Know your Teacher" session, Jenny took Chiara aside for a quiet talk about her name.

'Chiara, we've had to change your name to start in this new school. It's Keira now.'

'Why, Mummy? Why can't I be Chiara?'

'It's just a new rule we have to follow and Keira's not very different than Chiara is it? Can you do it?'

'But how will Daddy find me with a new name?'

Jenny sat back on her heels. She had forgotten how close Chiara had been to her father. Jenny hadn't mentioned his name for so long that she thought he'd been relegated to the back of Chiara's memory. Evidently this wasn't so. What could she say?

'Daddy will find you when he returns to Australia,' she said, hoping that no more questions would be asked.

Chiara thought for a moment. 'All right, Mummy. I like Keira anyway. I can be a new girl with a new name.'

'Okay.' Jenny hugged her daughter.

'I'll have to practice writing my new name,' Keira said, rushing off to find pens and paper, her queries about her daddy already forgotten.

Later, Jenny told Jed what had happened.

'You handled that rather well,' he said. 'Both with the principal and Chiara. We'd better start calling her Keira too.' He lifted her chin up so her eyes met his. 'Looks like I have a new girlfriend that lies like hell.'

'New? Who was the old one?' Jenny teased him, tickling him until their playfighting turned into a deep kiss.

'Never you mind,' he growled softly. 'Just feel lucky you are the new one.'

'Lucky am I? It's you who's lucky.'

Sometime later Jed tucked her arm into his, straightened his jeans and shirt, and walked out into the garden where Ryan was playing in the dirt and Chiara was busy at the outdoor table copying her name onto some A4 paper.

'We're both lucky, I think,' he said, as he gave her a squeeze.

'Yes,' breathed Jenny, squeezing him back.

Jenny smiled as she remembered that day. It had turned out very well indeed.

And now it was time for her and the new Keira to go into the classroom to meet the teacher.

There was only one room, decorated in a lovely manner. Jenny could see the children's names and pictures on the wall. The older children had written something about their families as well. The bookshelves were crammed with new and well-loved children's literature. On the desks were coloured pencils and crayons for the new children to draw a picture while the teacher talked to the mothers.

Jenny felt immediately at home. This was just the kind of classroom that she had taught in when she was younger.

She noticed Chiara was asked to sit next to another new girl at one of the smaller desks.

'Hello,' said the girl. 'What's your name?'

Jenny held her breath.

Chiara thought for a moment. 'I have a new name. It's Keira,' she said with a smile.

'Will you be my friend?' the girl asked.

'Okay,' said Keira, and they started to giggle together.

Jenny realised she was still holding her breath. She let it out in a whoosh.

'I guess it is a bit scary if this is your first child at school,' another mother said kindly, turning to her.

Jenny nodded. She could hardly speak. It seemed that everything was going to be all right. Not only that but maybe she had just made a new friend too.

Chapter 30

Jenny was passing the table in the hall when the phone rang.

'Hello,' she said.

'Hello, Ms Heath. It's Bill Docker, the school principal here.'

For a moment Jenny didn't recall who Ms Heath was, and then she remembered it was her.

'I'm ringing to advise you that I need the original birth certificate for Keira. Unfortunately I didn't notice that you had given me a copy. A member of the Education Department has phoned me and asked about the copy. I told him that you were a new parent and had just moved to the area so that he could understand how it happened. I hope you can get it to me asap.'

Jenny caught her breath. 'Who ... who was this person?' she stammered.

'Don't worry. It must just be a clerk in the department. I'm sure all will be well.'

'Thanks,' Jenny said. 'I'll get it to you as soon as I can.' She put the phone down, missing the cradle and letting it fall to the floor. Absently she picked it up and as she placed it on the cradle, it rang. Jenny stared at it. Could this be John? She was stunned by the idea that the forgery that she was involved in might be found out. Her fear connected her with her bigger fear. Could this be John phoning? Not likely, but even so she

194

dared not answer it. After five rings the message bank picked up.

'This is Vicki from the library. Exciting news! A friend of yours just saw your picture in the local paper and recognised you. He asked where you lived. Of course I didn't tell him – you know, confidentiality and all that.'

Jenny picked up the phone and pressed the open line button.

'Vicki, I'm here. I just got to the phone. What photo?'

'You know, Jenny, the one I took of you and the kids listening to a story at the library. The one with them all wide-eyed and enraptured as you read *Where the Wild Things Are.*'

'I didn't know you'd taken a picture,' Jenny squealed.

Vicki could hear the anxiety in Jenny's voice. 'Sorry, Jenny. I did tell you that we would be advertising the storytelling times and days in the local paper. I guess you didn't take it in. But all is well. The photos are lovely and it has led to a friend finding you. Isn't that great?'

'Thanks, Vicki, got to go.' Jenny hung up the phone. She was shaking badly.

Jenny knew the 'friend' must have been John. The two things to-gether – the call from the school and the man at the library – was too much of a coincidence for it not to be John. He was here and it wouldn't take long for him to find out where she lived and arrive without warning. He probably had a car and could be here any minute, she thought.

Jenny yelled to the kids. 'Come here, put your shoes on. We're going for a walk.'

'I don't want to go for a walk,' Chiara whined.

'Too bad,' Jenny yelled. She bent to pull on their shoes and strap the velcro.

'Come on.' She grabbed both their hands and almost ran out the door, leaving it open. She turned towards Jed's big house. *If I go along the fence line where the trees are he mightn't see me.*

The property stretched along the road. An electric fence was bounded by shade trees and shrubs that had been left to grow wild. The paddocks ran up the hill where cattle grazed. Anyone from the road would be able to see up the hill and would see them walking along. But if they kept close to the tree line they would be better protected.

Jenny started off at a run, dragging the kids along with her. But this didn't work and she soon had to stop the rush. The tree line had a lot of wombat holes that made it difficult to walk. The cattle also liked to walk the tree line and had created hoof holes in the muddy ground after it rained.

Soon Chiara and Ryan were refusing to go any further.

She had two choices. Climb the hill to a more even ground so that the children would be able to manage, or go down to the road and walk along the verge.

Jenny was so afraid. What if John came by in a car, saw them by the road and manhandled them into the car? What if he saw them on the hill running across to Jed's house and waited for them at the end of the paddock? All would be lost.

Her fear made her angry. 'Come on,' she yelled at them. She picked up Ryan and carried him for a few steps but he was too heavy to continue.

'Why are we hurrying, Mummy?' asked Chiara.

Jenny thought for a moment. 'Because there's a bad man who wants to grab us.' Jenny felt awful about saying this, especially if John did come by in his car. She didn't want the children to think badly about their father, even through all this trouble.

The kids began to puff and pant and Jenny kept swivelling her head around to see what was coming along the road. Several cars passed but they had locals she recognised in them.

Just before a bend in the road that hid her house from view she saw a car pull up into her driveway. It must be John. He would knock or even go inside as she had left the door open. He would find that she was not there.

She thought about what was in the house. She hadn't brought anything with her that would give anyone a clue to her past life. She had no photos of the children in the house. She had made their rooms look inviting with new posters of nursery rhymes and stories. He might not realise that it was her. He might think he had made a mistake. After all, photos in the local paper were notoriously fuzzy. Right? No, she was kidding herself. He was after her and the kids and she knew she wasn't safe.

They came to the alley, a thin strip of track that wove beside and between the paddocks, used to herd cattle from one paddock to another. The cattlemen would open a gate leading into the alley and herd the cattle to the next paddock where the grass was lush. It was a good method of ensuring none of the cattle drifted away from the herd and had to be herded again. The wire for the alley was not electrified and stands of trees grew along this fence line that had been planted by the local Land Care group.

Jenny held open two of the wires so the kids could climb through. The going was much smoother now and the trees would still hide them. The alley led straight up to the house which was surrounded by gravel and grass.

With a free grassy area to run on, Jenny and the kids took off to the shed where they could hear Jed tinkering with the truck.

'He's here. He's after us,' Jenny cried.

Jed took one look at Jenny and took action.

'Here, get in the truck and down on the floor. Cover yourselves with the dog rug.' Jenny and the kids moaned as the smelly dog rug was thrown over them. Even the kids obeyed as they could hear the fear in their mother's voice.

Just then a car came around the bend in the drive. A man got out. Jed did not know what John looked like and Jenny, who was hiding in the well of the truck, could not see or tell him.

Jed walked to the shed door with a spanner in his hand.

'Hey, can I help you?'

'Yes, can you tell me where the people who live in the house down there might be today?'

The man turned and pointed towards Jenny's house as he spoke. Jenny began to shake as she heard the voice. It was John.

She was afraid that the kids would hear their father's voice too and call out to him. She pulled them towards her, touched her forefinger to her lips to indicate that they must be quiet, and buried their heads in her arms and the rug. Ryan began to wriggle and pull away but with her heart pounding, she pulled him closer to her. Somehow the tension in her body alerted them to danger and they stayed still.

Jed took his time, cleaning the spanner with the cloth he had in his other hand before he replied.

'Nope, I rent the house but I don't keep an eye on them.'

John stood for a moment and thought about this.

'I thought they might come up to swim in your pool sometimes.' He gestured towards the pool visible at the rear of the house.

'Well, they have a couple of times but not lately. Guess they're busy with other things to do.'

John turned to go with a wave of his hand and Jed slowly walked back into the shed. It was just luck that he didn't yell out to Jenny in the truck, as just then John came back to the shed door.

It would be just like John not to trust Jed and come back to see if I'm here, Jenny thought.

Jed turned.

'I just thought of something. Does this road lead to other properties?'

'Yep,' said Jed. 'There are two other properties about 20 ks down the road and then it turns into the A4 main road.'

'Thanks,' John muttered.

'No worries,' Jed replied, and he watched John as he got into his car and left.

Chapter 31

'I guess that was John?'

Jenny nodded, looking sour.

'Stay in the truck. I'll get my wallet and phone.'

Jed leaned in. 'I've thought about what we would do if he showed up. I've got a friend in East Gippsland on the other side of Melbourne, Pete, who I've known since school, who has a property with tourist caravans and cabins on it. He said anytime we came by he and Liz would have a spot for us. I'll phone him as we go, and we're going now.'

'Now,' Jenny squeaked. 'What about … '

'There's no time. He'll be back and you might not be so lucky next time.'

After he'd gone into the house for his essentials, Jed jumped in the cab. Six scared eyes looked up at him from the well of the truck. He grinned.

'I'll tell you when you can sit up.'

He whistled for his dog, who jumped into the truck tray and stood with his face to the breeze.

Jed trundled down the drive to the road. There was no one in sight. He turned right and set off at the normal slow pace of the locals.

'What about the cattle? What about the house?'

'I'll phone Jack, the manager, who was going to move the cattle tomorrow, and tell him I'll be a few days. As for the house, Tilly comes tomorrow to clean so I can ask her to keep an eye out.'

Jed quickly made several calls. They drove a few kilometres down the road and saw no parked cars or even anyone on the road.

'I've fixed it with Pete and Liz in East Gippsland. As luck would have it, they have a spare cabin just right for you and the kids.'

As the truck hit the bitumen of the A4, Jed said, 'I think you can get up now.'

Jenny put her hand on Jed's arm. 'Thanks,' she said softly.

'Anything for my girl,' Jed murmured, glancing once at Jenny before looking back at the road.

Jenny smiled shyly. Even through this entire trauma she heard the words 'my girl' with a lift of her heart.

The kids bounced around. There were only two seat belts in the front of the cab. Jenny and Jed had one each so the kids were squeezed between them. It was an uncomfortable ride but what could they do? After another fifty kilometres, the kids were asleep despite the discomfort.

Jenny spoke quietly to Jed.

'Do you have to go back to the property straight away? We mightn't see you for a while.'

Jed looked down at Jenny. Her face looked miserable, her eyes sad.

'I can stay a few days. Jack can look after the cattle until next week when we need to cull for market. After that,' he shrugged, 'we'll see.'

Comforted, Jenny settled in and soon drifted off to sleep as well.

About five hundred kilometres further on, a lurch of the truck on a cattle grate woke her. She looked out the window and saw that the day had turned into night hours before and there was a house in the distance with lights in every window.

'Nearly there,' Jed said.

When they arrived she stayed put while Jed met his friends, who gave him a key to a cabin, and then he carried the children in to bed. Within a few minutes they were all asleep, safe and sound. Jed had stayed the night up at the main house, to relax with his mate over stories old and new.

The morning was bright and filled with bird calls. Jenny looked out the door of the cabin to a view of fields in every direction. Their cabin was one of five that stood on a small rise at the end of the property. Each cabin faced a different direction with a stand of pines and gums so there was a feeling of privacy. To the left was a recreation area with tennis courts, stables, a trampoline, a skateboard ramp and a pool. It was ideal for the kids. They were already up and exploring.

'Can we go for a horse ride now?' Chiara was impatient to get started on holiday fun.

'Not now,' Jenny sighed. 'Just let's settle in first.'

It wasn't long before Jed came bouncing down on a quad bike. Jenny met him at the front gravel section to the cabin.

'How was it?' he enquired. 'Sleep well?'

'Mm,' said Jenny, and gave him a kiss on the cheek.

Chiara who was standing at the front door said, 'Ooh, a mushy kiss.' Jenny and Jed laughed.

Jenny thought about how the kids were accepting Jed so well.

'Perhaps you can stay here tonight.'

Jed smiled and wiggled his eyebrows then, grabbing Ryan, hoisted him onto the quad bike and said, 'Let's go for a ride, mate.'

The rest of the day was spent trying all the recreation areas of the property and buying in food and a few essentials from the local village shops.

Jenny phoned her mum and dad on her pre-paid mobile.

'Dad, John came close to finding us and it was only through Jed's quick thinking that we escaped and are now safe in a cabin in East Gippsland, a place called Morwell.'

Jenny gave them the details of what had happened, after Mac had turned up the sound on his phone and held it up for Lilli to listen to the story as well. The gasps and worried voices almost had Jenny in tears again. At last Jed came to the phone and reassured Lilli and Mac about how safe they all were. Jenny was last on the phone.

'I'll be okay, Dad. We'll just have to figure out what to do next.'

Jed stood outside on the verandah looking at the stars. What would the children think of his sleepover with Jenny tonight, he wondered?

As if in answer to his thought, a little hand slid into his. He looked down to see Chiara's eyes gazing up at him from the light inside.

'Daddy is a long way away, isn't he?'

Jed found his voice caught in his throat. He just nodded.

'I love Daddy.'

Jed crouched down to look into Chiara's eyes and said, 'And he loves you too, sweetheart.'

'Mummy was sad when Daddy was at home.'

'Yes, she was.'

'Mummy is happy now you're here.'

Jed choked on his reply, pulled Chiara close to him in a big hug, then lifted her up onto his shoulders and turned to the door.

'Mind your head,' he said softly, as they went inside to where Jenny and Ryan were waiting.

Chapter 32

We realised that John was back in Sydney when we spotted the blue Mazda again.

We knew he'd found Jenny and the kids even though he'd lost them again soon after. How did he find them? What connections did he have that could allow him access to their confidential files?

I thought of Richard and how he had been able to hack into the police files. I supposed people who were experts in computer work might be able to do it.

Now we knew he had found them, why was he hanging around us?

The answer seemed to be: revenge.

He had taken to letting us see him now. He was not hiding. He was out in the open.

This could have made things better – no surprises. But it didn't. We began looking behind us at every turn and scanning the area for a glimpse of him. He must have known that we'd spoken to Jenny and he must have been confident that if he could find her once, he could find her again. Sometimes I caught him looking directly into my eyes and smiling a rather sinister smile. I was petrified. This stalking seemed more threatening than before. We went to the police again.

'There's nothing we can do unless you have proof of stalking. He has a right to be in the same places as you,' was the answer we got from them. It didn't seem right.

Every time we saw John we rang the police. Eventually we were put onto a higher authority at the station.

'Chief Inspector Hughes here. I believe you are having stalking incidents?'

Mac explained what had been happening with the stalker.

'There are new laws about stalking which must not have filtered down to the administration. I'll put you in touch with the Domestic Violence Liaison Officers. They will be out to see you either today or tomorrow.' This seemed better.

We felt a little relieved. By the end of the day a Ms Rebecca Dawson visited us.

She pushed her glasses further up onto her nose and started a discussion about the new laws regarding stalking. First, she told us that most stalkers are men and most victims are women, especially women who have experienced or recently left an abusive relationship. Since 2007 stalking has become a crime under an Australia-wide Act.

'That is, if a person has the intention of causing physical or mental harm, arousing apprehension or fear to a victim, and has a persistent course of conduct they are liable to police action,' she quoted from the statute.

Ms Dawson was full of information.

'It seems that the desk officers who have spoken to you were not aware of the Act well enough to help you. That will be dealt with immediately. However it is true that proof is needed to apprehend these people. You saying they were there is not enough proof, as they could have many reasons that would sound reasonable to the judge about why they were there, and your case would fail. This is especially true of your case, as it is your ex-son-in-law and the consensus might be that your daughter may have influenced your minds to think badly of him. This would be the tack a defending lawyer would take in the case and could win. Statistics today show that just over half of all cases have not been proven or the perpetrator has received a suspended sentence.'

'What can we do then, to help our case, Ms Dawson?' I asked.

'The most useful idea is to keep a "Stalking Incident Log". Here, I'll show you an example of one.'

She spread out a large office style hard cover book that was divided into sections. We noted the date, time, place, as well as who was stalking, what they were doing, how long they were there, who else was in the vicinity, and what action the victim took. It was very comprehensive.

'This would become a record of the stalking, to prove from your perspective, that the stalking was persistent, caused mental harm and aroused fear in you.'

'Why do you say "from our perspective," Ms Dawson?' Mac enquired.

'It is important to realise that the judge will be impartial and will wonder if you are making up these sightings because you have a grudge against this person. To counter this issue, a good idea is to take a photo that has a date stamp on it. This will prove the stalker's persistence and match your log.'

Mac and I nodded. Everything she had advised seemed excellent and we were ready to start. I found an unused book and our camera. We checked that it had a date feature on it. We were ready to act.

Within a week John had stalked us three times. I diligently wrote down the report in our log while Mac took a photo each time. We became aware that the photo needed to be taken without John's knowledge. If he was aware of our actions he might try to hide more effectively so that we could not catch him. We needed those photos.

I wondered how long we would need to keep this log before it was considered persistent, so I phoned Rebecca Dawson to ask.

'There's no hard and fast rule,' she advised. 'But I think a couple of months may be sufficient. When you feel that your log book shows persistence, then come into the office and we will have our police prosecutor look at it and help us decide if this would be enough to go forward with the case.'

I rang Tony and Samantha and also Jenny to say what had been advised. They were all happy that something was being done. They hadn't realised that the stalking laws in Australia had changed. We all agreed that this should be advertised more than it was so that victims would feel less helpless and perpetrators would be less inclined to stalk others.

I whispered that the paparazzi should be added to the list of stalkers as I was always annoyed that celebrities could be hounded so much. I wondered if, in the Princess Diana case, the paparazzi could be sued for causing physical harm. Probably not, I thought, as this law was very new and perhaps was not yet a law in Britain.

At last, for the first time since our ordeal had begun, Mac and

I felt we were in control. We had something positive to do. I wished we'd known about stalking earlier on. Maybe we could have started this sooner.

But, as it turned out, we didn't get to finish the log before something else happened to change our resolve.

Chapter 33

My ukulele group, Sydney North Ukulele Gang (SNUGS), was invited to play a gig on the forecourt of the Opera House.

This was a major event for us. The Sydney Opera House had been designed by Jorn Utzon, a Danish architect, who had won an international design competition in the late 50s. Today the building is acclaimed as a UNESCO World Heritage Site. Unfortunately, the government of the day didn't fully appreciate the costs and work involved and a dispute arose, with Utzon resigning and the building being completed in 1973 under the direction of the government architect Peter Hall. Now everyone in Sydney is proud of our Opera House and it's quite a privilege to perform there.

We were only playing in the forecourt, not the main theatre, on the point of land named after Bennelong, an indigenous man who was a guide to the land for our early white settlers. Still, our group was ecstatic that we'd received the invitation to play. So far we'd only played at local venues on the northern beaches. Now the Opera House forecourt. Very flash!

We were to perform from 6pm to 7pm, before a younger crowd would arrive and take over the floor with dancing to live rock music. Everyone in our group was on time to meet the hired bus at the designated stop. Mac came with me, as did a number of partners of ukulele members.

Once we had set up our music stands and tuned our instruments we had time to look around. The stage was slightly elevated from the dance floor with tables for customers surrounding it. The nearby bar and restaurant was doing a roaring trade, as was the sushi bar further down the walkway.

There were at least 300 people there. It seemed to me to be the biggest pickup joint in town.

It was certainly the most beautiful. The walkway led to the Opera House, its sails shining in the setting sun.

Across the harbour were small craft, bobbing in the bays. Luna Park was lit up and we could see the ferris wheel turning and even hear faint screams from the opposite shore as people reached the top and were plunged down the other side.

The concourse street lights brightened around the area as evening closed in. Opposite the forecourt, the Harbour Bridge loomed over the dark water as many yachts headed home. A cruise ship looked magnificent as it glittered at its overseas terminal berth.

People were strolling out from the underground carpark in a variety of dress. Some were in evening clothes going to the opera or ballet. Some were obviously tourists, probably from the ship at the overseas terminal as they had backpacks, cameras and maps and occasionally we could hear a too-loud American accent.

Mac had managed to score a beer from a harried waitress and was sitting at a table sipping his drink. He arched his eyebrows at me and nodded to the left.

A gaggle of twenty-somethings was tottering towards him. They had bandage dresses on that certainly looked up to their name. They looked as if they could only have been bandaged in hospital by a competent nurse from chest to high thigh. They wore platform shoes or ankle boots that made their legs seem to be longer than the rest of their bodies. They could hardly walk and most had to keep their knees slightly bent so they could move with the required wriggle.

It was time to do our gig. The leaders of SNUGS were great players and singers. They held the floor at the front while I and other players strummed at the back, adding voice and sound to the group. It was such fun I even forgot my woes for a time.

After each song the audience whooped and clapped. They were really getting into it. They were also getting more inebriated. A few were singing and some were even dancing to the music. We felt quite chuffed that we were doing so well.

We'd decided to play our Beatles and rock 'n roll set, add Abba's *Mama Mia*, the Village People's *YMCA*, and *Georgie Girl* from the Seekers. We concluded with two older numbers, *Singing the Blues* and *Alexander's Rag Time Band* in fast time and a flourish, and received a hearty clap that made us feel very satisfied. While the leaders took down the mics and stands, I joined Mac at his table and began to seriously peruse the company.

There was group of men with baggy trousers and backward-facing peaked caps nearby. There were overdressed fifty-something women with thick cake makeup and very red lips. There were girls flashing plump thighs and extra low cleavage.

Then, there was John.

I took a breath and grabbed Mac.

'Over there near the bar,' I said out of the corner of my mouth. 'No, don't look now.' Then, 'Look now.'

Mac was shocked. There was John at the bar with a rather glamorous bandaged body. Mac and I ducked our heads behind our hands. I pulled my ukulele stage hat down over my forehead.

John's hands had wandered down the woman's back to slap her bottom. He looked very comfortable with her. She turned to give him a kiss and they stayed locked this way for the longest time.

I could feel myself getting angry. How dare he! He was married to Jenny. He had two children. He said he wanted her back. He was harassing us because he thought we had taken her.

I stood up.

Mac grabbed my arm. I flung his arm away and raced forward to where John was standing.

I screamed at him. 'How dare you! How dare you! Who do you think you are? You have a wife and kids who are missing and you are out with this … this floozy.'

Out of the corner of my eye I could see that Ms Bandaged Body looked shocked by my words, and then angry at me calling her a floozy. And why wouldn't she, I realised afterwards? But in the heat of the moment I had my back up. She stepped back out of the way and left John to cope with me on his own.

The other people in his immediate group also stepped away and were looking at him curiously.

The blood that had rushed to my head was allowing me to keep up the tirade of words.

'Do you really care what happens to Jenny? Do you? Why are you out having fun and with another woman when for all you know, Jenny may need your help?'

I was really into it now, even forgetting that we had helped Jenny to escape and had hidden her and, of course, didn't need or want his help.

He leant towards me and looked into my eyes. 'I will get you for this,' he said quietly.

I pointed my finger at him ready to start another tirade of words, when Mac grabbed my arm again and hauled me away. I stumbled back and down the step behind me. I was still shouting at John. 'You are such a nasty and horrible person.'

The last I saw of John, he was trying to explain to his friends what had just happened.

Mac kept tugging me until we had cleared the dance and seating area.

As the bus wouldn't leave for another 30 minutes, he hurried me around the Opera House walkway to the wharf, where we caught a ferry to Manly, then a taxi home. By this time my anger had subsided. I was now feeling guilty over what I'd done. His last words were echoing in my brain.

'What have I done?' I wailed at Mac.

He just hugged me until I stopped moaning.

'This has got to stop,' he said at last. We agreed that we needed to find more help from somewhere. Anywhere.

Chapter 34

In my mind I kept replaying the conversation I'd had with John, all night and most of the next day. A horrible habit that I couldn't get rid of.

It was about 4pm when something happened to make me forget.

'What's been left on, out on the verandah?' I asked Mac.

'Nothing that I know of. But I can smell smoke.'

We hurried down the hall to the verandah room at the back. Neither of us smoked and there was no reason for a heater to be on in hot weather.

Smoke was pouring through the back door screen, and as we peered into the room, we could see that licks of flame had caught the curtains and furniture nearby, as well as the rug and the wood around the nearest windows. The heat was so intense that we had to step back to breathe. The smoke was now billowing into the rest of the house through the open hall door where we were standing. A few sparks landed near our feet and we couldn't see further than a couple of metres in front of our noses.

'We've got to get out,' Mac yelled. 'Shut the hall door.'

I banged the door shut just as the fire alarm went off in the kitchen. Its piercing scream only heightened our fears.

As we ran down the hall, smoke was coming thick and fast under the hall door that we'd just closed. Flames began to shoot up the walls in the hall. It was getting hard to breathe and to see in front of us. Thank goodness the hall led straight to the front door.

Once there, I fumbled to open it, and saw it had been locked with a device on the inside. I flicked the switch and slammed the door back against the wall as we tumbled out. We both took deep clear breaths of air and just looked at each other, stunned. We were lucky to be alive, we realised, having seen so many television shows about fire and how it only took four minutes to burn down a house with everyone in it.

Mac was busy phoning 'Triple 0' on his mobile, which he'd grabbed from the hall table as we'd run outside, so I rushed around the side of the house to the hose. I turned it on and sprayed it full bore over the side walls of the verandah. Then I gave it to Mac while I hurried around to the garden where another hose was coiled near the vegetable patch. I drenched the back of the house where most of the damage had been done, but couldn't stay there for long as the heat was so intense.

Our neighbour on the left came out to see what was happening and quickly hosed his side of our house and the fence between.

Within five minutes the fire brigade turned up and began spraying foam on the whole house. Their expertise soon had the fire out, leaving a mass of wet foamy walls and a muddy garden.

The fire chief came over to us.

'How did this start?'

Mac and I shook our heads, feeling helpless. We had no idea.

'Don't go inside until we've had a good look around. We need to establish how the fire started and if it's been properly extinguished,' was his instruction to us.

We stood in our front garden – although one could no longer call it a garden as all the plants had been trampled to the ground and everything was muddy, with large holes where the firefighters had trodden. Still, we were alive, and that was what counted.

After a while the fire chief came back to speak to us. He looked quite stern and rather angry.

'The fire was purposely lit. There is evidence of petrol and rags under the back room footings. There'll have to be an enquiry. Do you know of anyone who would hate you enough to do this?'

Of course we knew who could hate us this much! Mac and I looked at each other. Should we say who we thought it was? Would this just bring more revenge down upon our heads?

Mac took the lead for which I was grateful as I couldn't make up my mind what was best to do.

'I don't think so,' he said. 'Maybe your investigation will turn up some clues.'

The fire chief nodded and returned to his truck to start writing a laptop report. Everyone in our little street was outside our house. Most people looked relieved that their homes were no longer in danger. Some looked sad for us and our damage. Little by little they came to speak to us and offer their condolences and then drifted away home now the excitement was over.

The fire chief was the last to leave, informing us about what would happen now. Evidently the report would go to head office and we would be receiving details of the investigation and our role in it. He also gave us a list of people to contact who would be available to clean up the mess and restore the inside to a habitable state. Neither Mac nor I dared to speak about our insurance cover and whether we'd be covered if the fire was found to have been deliberately lit. We just couldn't face the prospect.

We wandered through the house looking in each room. The front of the house had not been damaged by fire but was completely water-logged. Most of the furniture looked like it would need to be replaced, along with pictures, cushions and curtains.

When we got to the kitchen, next to the verandah, we saw that this section of the house had only a skeleton of black frame left.

I rushed back to the bedroom at the front and opened the water-logged wardrobe. Were our family photo albums still intact? They were certainly there but looked very wet. I took them out to the front porch and spread them out. Maybe if I got the sun on them straight away the damage would be minimal.

Jean called out from across the road.

'Would you like to come over for a rest and a cup of tea?'

We accepted gratefully, comforted by the fact that we had neighbours who were such good friends. I gathered up the photo albums and took them with me. I didn't want to leave them out there alone.

We sat in Jean's sunroom. The windows looked out onto our house across the street, and the view was forlorn. Already, I didn't feel this was our home any more. I knew Mac was thinking the same.

Payback, I thought. I knew this had been caused by John. He was so angry on the day I accosted him at the Opera House. I had made him look foolish in front of the woman he had with him and his friends. 'I will get you for this,' he'd said. After the terror of the fire and the shock of finding this was arson, I just knew it was John. Of course I had no real proof, not unless the investigators came up with some evidence.

I remembered that John's mother had said that he'd set their house alight when he hadn't got his own way and had nearly burnt his father to death. It was only his mother returning home who'd woken the father and got him out of the house in time. After he lit that fire, he may have hung around so he could see how upset his mother and father had been. So too on this occasion. He could have been here among the people who came from several streets away to see our fire. It wasn't hard to imagine that John had done it again.

I hoped investigators would find some evidence, finger prints or something like that, which would point to John and take him away from us. This was not just harassment any more. This was life and death. This was a crime.

I was so tired yet angry as well. It was only tiredness that stopped me from screaming and yelling and hitting out at anything in my way. Mac could tell how I felt and he took my hand.

I tried to disengage my hand but he held it firmly. He rubbed his thumb up and down my wrist and smiled tiredly down at me. His face was covered in black sooty streaks.

'I know what you think. I feel the same way. But at this moment I'm alive and so are you. The house was just bricks and wood. It's not us.'

I knew he was right. But still. I loved that home where all our memories were.

'We can build new memories,' Mac said as if he knew what I was thinking.

I felt such guilt. 'It was my fault. If I hadn't yelled at John and called him names in front of his friends he might not have taken this revenge.'

Mac was more rational.

'He's been building up to this all along. First, it was just harassment and annoyance, then it was stunts to get us upset, then trolling, and now it's a fire. It's not your fault, Lilli. He's to blame and only him.'

I sat on the bed in Jean's spare room, where she'd offered us a place for the night. I was so tired, I lay down on the bed in the clothes I was wearing and closed my eyes. I felt Mac covering me with the quilt and tiptoeing out. I knew he'd thank Jean for letting us stay.

The next morning I was disoriented when I woke. Then it all came back to me in a wave, like a tsunami. Mac was already awake and smiling at me.

'I've already phoned Jenny and Tony about the fire. They're very upset for us and will help in any way they can, they say. But this is the start of a new day. A new life!'

I hugged him. Thank goodness for my husband's strength and calmness. It was exactly what I needed to get up off the bed.

Chapter 35

Jean told us to use her landline phone for the insurance company, as we knew the call would take some time. Mac arranged to meet a representative on the site of the fire that afternoon.

The assessor was a young man, aged about twenty, and it seemed to be almost his first job. He explained that because the fire had been classified as arson, the company wouldn't be able to pay out any funds. Not unless the conclusion of the enquiry was in our favour.

I was annoyed.

'Why? Where are we going to live, and how will we deal with the mess?'

'We'll be talking to the local police and the fire brigade. Then we'll decide if the arson was self-inflected, that is carried out by either of you, or not, and ...'

'You think we set fire to our own house so that we would have nowhere to live?' By now I was furious.

The assessor looked a bit ashamed and cleared his throat.

'There are many types of people out there.' He pointed out into the world. 'They set fire to their homes to claim insurance and go on a holiday or buy cheaply somewhere else.'

I figured it was pointless to take him on over hypotheticals.

'So where will we live while you decide?'

'You need to find a rental property that accommodates you for at least two weeks until the decision has been made. If we agree to pay out on the insurance, then you will need to find accommodation that fits with our policy as far as cost goes. It would be best to find a place now that fits our rental fees so that you don't have to move again if we agree to a payout.'

There was nothing we could do. Mac rang the insurance company and complained to the manager. We felt that the assessor they had sent out was meant to bear the brunt of our anger, so they wouldn't have to deal with complaints.

Jean listened to our story.

'You can stay here,' she offered, a little reluctantly.

'No,' said Mac. 'It's better if we can just use your computer to find a hotel for the night and then a suitable rental for the future. Then we'll be out of your hair straight away. We're not good company right now, Jean. We just want to crawl away into a hole and lick out wounds. You understand … '

It wasn't long before we'd found a place a few streets away from our street and in the right money bracket. We went around to see it immediately. It was clean, modern and available the next day. It would do.

Then we went out to buy some essentials. Thank goodness our cars had been out on the street when the fire occurred or we might have lost them too in the general damage that had occurred. As it was, we still felt we had nothing. There was nothing to salvage. A few sticks of furniture could be rubbed up and painted again, that was all. The one good thing, I joked to Mac, was that the computer had been destroyed so we wouldn't be tempted to look at the blog.

Mac and I organised a new computer and a gmail account at an internet café and gave our new address to all our internet friends we could think of. We also advised the police and insurance company of our new address. A few days later the police came around to the rental property.

'Our normal policy is to take surreptitious photos or videos of the crowd at a fire, as firebugs like to watch,' they told us.

That meant another trip to the local police station so we could view the pictures. At first the crowd consisted of our neighbours. We gave the police assurances that they either lived next door or a few doors down. But as the fire took hold, we noticed the arrival of a number of people who just seemed to like to watch a tragic happening. At the back of the crowd I saw a familiar face. He had a cap on and glasses and was moving from group to group as a means of hiding. I gasped and then looked at Mac. The police picked up on my expression straight away.

'Who did you see just then?'

They played the video back a short way and watched us carefully as they moved it forward frame by frame. I couldn't keep control over my expression when we came to the pictures of John.

'Who is it?' Who's hiding in the background that you know who is not a regular visitor?'

This was the opportunity to tell them about John, or at least part of what we knew about him – but I feared the consequences.

'That's our son-in-law, John. He doesn't live around here and in fact our daughter has left him.'

The police glanced at each other.

'This may be a motive for the arson. We'll need to look into it. I noticed that you have a file here at the station about harassment and stalking. Do you think it's this person, the same one who is stalking you?'

Mac answered, 'He may be the one. But surely he wouldn't set fire to our house?'

The police took out our file and speed-read through it again. They snapped it closed and ushered us out without telling us what they would do.

At the door Mac turned back to ask a question.

'If it is our son-in-law, my wife and I are concerned that he will try something else. Can you do something to protect us?'

One of the detectives sighed.

'We can take out a restraining order against him so that he can't come within a hundred yards of you and your establishment. We can arrange drive-by cars to your property at various times during the day and night. And we can caution him to stay away. That's about all we can do unless we find proof that he was involved in the arson. Then he would be charged.'

We thanked them and left, knowing full well that these measures wouldn't really protect us at all. We'd had police drive-by vehicles before and they hadn't worked. We were unsure what John might do but we were certain he would do something. He'd never give up.

....

Everything was quiet for a week. The insurance company still hadn't made a decision and Mac was worried that we wouldn't be recompensed. Money was tight, especially as we'd already lost $31,000 on the false identity fiasco.

On Wednesday evening we heard the screech of a car, a door slamming and a pounding on our front door. If we'd expected it to be John, we probably would have hidden inside and not answered the door. As it was, we opened the door straight away only to see John, having opened the wire screen door, standing there glowering at us.

'How dare you set the police onto me. They treated me like a criminal and have taken my finger prints and shoe prints.'

Mac retaliated. 'You were there at the fire, we saw you. What were you doing there if not to ruin our house?'

'I was coming to see you and that's what I told the police. Now get out of my life before I do something that could really hurt you.'

He smashed the wire screen door closed so hard it bounced straight back at him as he ran down the steps.

I felt very concerned. The words he'd spoken seemed to imply that he didn't start the fire. Maybe he was just coming to see us? I mentioned my fears to Mac as soon as John had gone.

'John hasn't been to "see us" since the very first time almost one year ago. He has been harassing us, stalking us and causing trouble for most of that time. He has created a nasty blog that could have destroyed our peace. Do you really think he's innocent? I'm glad the police went around to see him. Perhaps now he'll be frightened enough to desist. Besides – how did he know we were here in the rental? We've only been here for two weeks and hardly anyone knows where we are.'

I'd forgotten that and now I could see that I realised I was too soft. Of course he was the one.

Mac rang the police to inform them of John's visit. The detective said he was sorry that John had become so intrusive and threatening. They had told him it was routine to take finger prints and shoe prints when arson was involved. The detective then said that the outcome of the case was inconclusive and that they had advised the insurance company of that decision.

'What about John?' queried Mac.

'There was no real evidence,' the detective said. After a few promises that they would keep looking into the case if new evidence came to light, he ended the call with us none the wiser about our financial position.

The next day the insurance company rang. They'd approved our claim. We could begin building a new home because their assessment had concluded that our old home, even though it still had habitable rooms, was more expensive to repair than to bulldoze and start again. They would also be paying for the rental property.

What a sense of relief!

Chapter 36

If we thought the only consequence of telling the police that John had been at the fire was that he would come around to scream us, we were wrong.

The real consequence was swift and frightening.

We'd been for a walk along the seaside walkway from Long Reef Beach to Dee Why Beach and were approaching the last bend before home. The sea was sparkling in the sun and to my eyes, the waves were tiny horses galloping and tumbling onto the beach.

On one side of the ocean bay there was a rocky cliff face that smelt of red clay and on the other side the land dropped away in rocky fingers from the walkway's wooden railing to the beach below.

There were a few families down on the beach and a row of surf board riders sitting out in the deep, waiting for the best wave. From where we were, they all looked tiny.

Suddenly I saw two figures looming towards us. Mac had noticed them first and grunted. I looked up and saw the two men in WWII great coats and boots over jeans and T-shirts. One had pierced lips, ears and eyebrows, and the other was short and stocky with tattoos on his neck and on all we could see of his arms, his wrists. I suspected he was the same person who had accosted me in the carpark. I couldn't see if he had a lion tattooed on his left hand because it was in his pocket.

They looked seriously bad.

Both of them were carrying something made of metal that looked like a spanner or car jack. They began tapping them on their other up-turned cupped hands. I caught a glimpse of that tattooed lion as the short guy turned his hand over.

Mac stopped. I looked behind me. There had been a few people walking along the walkway before, but none of them were here now. Mac quietly took his mobile out and dialled 000. Placing it to his ear he said, 'I've got the police emergency online if you come a step closer to us.'

The two men sneered, looked at each other and then one moved like lightning, swiping the phone out of Mac's hand. It landed on the ground and he jumped up and down on it as we heard the voice on the other end of the phone saying, 'Tell me the emergency?'

As Mac's phone was being crunched underfoot, Mac turned to run away, pushing me in front of him. I hardly needed a push to run but we were too late. Pierced Eyebrows nipped around in front of us, whilst Tattoo Man stayed behind us. There was no room to move.

'We're here to give you a final warning,' said Pierced Eyebrows in a chillingly scary, gravelly voice.

'Yeah,' echoed Tattoo Man. 'Keep away from Mr Stanford. Don't tell the police anything about him if you value your lives.'

They glared at us for a few seconds – which felt like minutes – and then turned and left, with Pierced Eyebrows giving Mac a last push against the railing of the walkway as he passed.

Mac careened off the railing as I reached for his arm. Some of the walkway's red earth crumbled away down the rocky slope as his foot slipped under the bottom of the railing. He managed to catch the railing with one arm and swing himself around to stumble back across the path, before he fell against the cliff on the other side of the track.

I followed him to the cliff face, and as he sank down to the concrete, I sat with him. Mac's chest was heaving and he was trying to catch his breath. The sound was harsh in the midst of the quiet air of soft sighing waves.

The men had disappeared. We couldn't even hear their footsteps on the walkway. I was shaking badly and even Mac was unsteady as he pulled himself up and stood by the railing, holding on with clenched hands.

After some minutes, we were able to move. We tottered home on shaky legs and sighed with relief when we were safe inside with the door locked.

Mac was so angry he could hardly speak. I knew he felt emasculated – shocked that he was unable to protect himself or me.

The fact that the men had grabbed his phone so quickly horrified him.

Mac said nothing. He sat in his chair in the lounge and closed his eyes. I went over and stood behind his chair, wrapping my arms around him.

'My hero,' I said. 'No one could have done anything more than you did.'

'It wasn't enough,' came the soft reply.

That evening Mac wasn't well. He didn't say anything at first but then admitted to feeling dizzy and headachy. I called the doctor.

'Blood pressure's up. I think an overnight stay in hospital will bring it down again.'

Hospital seemed a bit extreme, but better safe than sorry, I thought. Mac didn't argue, so he must have still felt unsure of himself. I helped Mac pack a bag and we drove to Mona Vale Hospital. After he had been admitted, I stayed until 10pm then set off for home. I hadn't liked to tell Mac how afraid I was to go home alone. He had enough to worry about. I parked in the garage and eventually got up the courage to open the front door. I locked it after me and went from room to room turning on all the lights, locking or checking all the windows and doors and checking under the beds and in the wardrobes. All the time I kept looking over my shoulder, frightened that someone was creeping up to grab me.

I took my mobile phone to bed with me programmed with the 'Triple 0' number. Under the blankets I also had with me a heavy vase from the lounge and a butcher's knife from the kitchen. I left every light in the house on and didn't care if any of the neighbours who might happen to look my way during the night thought I was crackers. I didn't even undress. I just took off my shoes. I was as ready as I could be for anything. Eventually I fell into a deep sleep.

In the morning I quickly washed my face and hands and had a croissant with apricot jam and a cup of tea before setting off for the hospital.

Mac was sitting up in bed, looking fine. The doctor had been around and advised that he could go home as long as he took it easy. As if …

We drove home, not even discussing the main issue that we had.

We couldn't talk about it just yet. I pottered around at home, keeping my eye on Mac who was resting on the lay-back chair with magazines, drinks and the TV remote to hand. Eventually we began to discuss what to do next.

I rang the police and told them what had happened, they arrived, and soon after, we all sat in the lounge room to tell our tale.

'It was all so quick,' I said. 'And then they were gone.'

My impression of WWII great coats, boots over jeans, and T-shirts – one man with pierced lips, ears and eyebrows and the other with tattoos on his neck and down his arms – was not substantial enduring identification. But the lion on the wrist of one of the men was specific enough to be useful.

'I could really only remember the metal spanners or car jacks they held menacingly in their hands,' was Mac's contribution.

The police dutifully took down these details but both Mac and I knew that we hadn't been much help at all. I wondered if the police could find or recognise these two by the piercings and tattoos but I mostly felt that they wouldn't be able to proceed very far with the small amount of information we 'd been able to give them.

We ended up at the police station again looking through books of likely criminals or bullies that lived in the area especially those with tattoos. We couldn't find a match. I added the incident of these two accosting us to a new log book as the other had been burnt in the fire. John must have paid them to accost us.

He was warning us off, I was sure of it. Pushing us to move away from the area, in the hope that we'd lead him to Jenny.

Chapter 37

The next ukelele gig at the Opera House was due that week. I wondered if I should take part in it, as I remembered what had happened the last time.

But Mac's view was, 'You know you love to play and be part of the gigs. It'll take your mind off things too.'

So we set off again to the outdoor forecourt area of the Opera House, opposite the Bridge and the overseas terminal. There were no ships at the terminal this time, but ferries arrived and set off again from the wharves, choofing over the harbour to the zoo or Manly.

I played exceptionally well, even though I hadn't practiced as much as I should have, and as we walked back to the carpark I was feeling very pleased with myself. Mac could tell I was pleased and grinned at me.

We'd just paid our parking fee and taken a ticket when suddenly a woman staggered towards us. She seemed familiar. Then I realised that it was the same woman who'd been with John when we were last there. I really only recognised her because she was wearing the same bandaged dress as last time.

She was extremely drunk, weaving all over the place. I wondered how she could stay upright on those very high heels. Even in my younger days I would not have been able to walk a straight line.

She barrelled up the slope towards the carpark entry, her head down. Then, close to us now, she looked up and hesitated.

'You!' she gasped. 'You were the one who made John angry and called me names.'

I stared at her and wondered how to answer. Should I apologise for making her look and feel a fool by calling her a floozy? In the end, I thought, I don't care. She was with John and maybe she's just as bad as him. Then I thought this might be a way to find out more about John and where he worked.

'Yes,' I said. 'How is he?'

Her shoulders slumped and her mouth screwed up angrily.

'I don't know. He's been sacked for hacking into government sites at work and also for turning up drunk once too often.'

'Oh,' I replied. 'Are you and he still ... ?' I waved my hand in the air to help her finish the end of the sentence for me.

'No way! I left him when he became too unstable and a bit violent. I haven't seen him since I left.'

'How was he violent?' I asked.

'He tried to hit me because I wouldn't do what he wanted me to. I wasn't going to stand for that. So I walked out. Besides, I didn't want to be with someone who was dishonest. He'll be in prison one day if he keeps on hacking into company files.'

Making a quick turn that swivelled her around so that she was facing the wrong way, then peering at the wall in front of her and swivelling back again, she weaved her way over to a group in the forecourt that looked like the same people as last time, and picked up a drink.

She was welcomed into the group by two of the men who threw their arms around her and gave her sloppy kisses on her cheeks. We could see that they were happy to see her and I guessed they were high-flying IT executives in Armani suits cooling down after work.

Mac and I looked at her for moment or two and then turned to walk into the carpark. Now we thought we knew how John had found Jenny. It was by hacking into the government schools website, and he'd been caught doing it. We hoped that now he was not at that job, he'd have less opportunity to hack into other government sites.

Would he get another job easily? To me, the IT community seemed to be very close-knit. Maybe word would spread that he was a hacker and he would find it difficult to find another honest job. IT people in the regular business world would need to have a great deal of honesty and integrity to work with their clients.

'Seems like John has been drinking a bit too much,' Mac observed. 'Hope that doesn't make him more violent.' I hoped not, as well.

In an instant, I felt sorry for Ms Bandaged Body. She'd obviously made a mistake in dating John and didn't realise it for a while.

Thank goodness she'd the sense to leave him before she became too entrapped, as our Jenny had been. Perhaps I'd even had a hand in the woman leaving him.

I grinned at Mac as I squeezed his arm.

'I think we might have done Ms Bandaged Body a favour, by helping her get rid of John.'

Chapter 38

Jed was crouched down by the tractor parked in the shed, when he heard a car door slam. John came up the winding drive.

'You're a liar,' he yelled and stopped menacingly in front of Jed, breathing heavily.

Jed stood up, a wrench still in his hands. John looked to be in a furious state.

'I went back to town and discovered that you and my wife had been seen together. You'd told me you didn't know much about who had rented the property down the hill and now I find out you're out with my wife.'

My. Wife. He spat out each word. 'Get out of my life and leave us alone.'

Jed looked calmly at John and, rather than join in a shouting match with him that could easily escalate into a fight, he just walked away further into the shed. Jed had assumed a calm demeanour but, even so, his fists were clenched in the effort not to land a punch on this brute of a man.

John turned to the shed door and strode out banging his fist on the wood beside the door as he left.

Jed waited a while until he thought John might have gone, and then walked out to the drive to see if the car had left. There was no sign of it. He breathed a sigh of relief. He didn't see what John could do, as Jenny wasn't there any longer.

It was a cloudless day and the cattle were in need of new feed. Jed and his manager, Jack, spent the time herding the cattle to a new paddock, forking hay for the vealers ready for sale, and checking the fences.

It was a very productive day, and Jed was tired when he finally returned to the house. He immediately went into the study to send an email to Jenny about John's visit. He stood looking down at the computer. He was sure he had turned it off before he went out. He moved the mouse to see what program it was on, but only his usual screen saver, with Jenny and the kids came up.

Jed was slightly worried, as the house had been open all day as was usual in the country, and John had known Jed was out working. He moved the cursor to recent documents. There on the screen was a record of recent action with his emails. He moved to his email account. There were at least a dozen emails to and from Jenny and his mate Pete's tourist company in Gippsland. If John had seen these and was as savvy as he seemed to be, he could have found out the address they were sent to. Jed couldn't risk it.

He had to phone Jenny now and tell her to get moving. He tried over and over again, but her phone was off the hook, maybe. It wasn't until 6pm that he was able to get through to her.

'It's Jed. You've got to get out of there NOW.'

'Jed,' Jenny's voice was confused, 'Why? What's happened?'

'John was here. He came into the house when I was out and saw my emails to you, and from Pete at the caravan camp, which has his address on all the company correspondence. I don't know how early John was in the house. He saw me at 9am, so he's had all day to find out and drive the five hours to your place. He could be there now. You need to get out. Find a motel in town near the station and catch a train back to me. Perhaps he won't think that you would return so quickly.'

Jenny inhaled deeply. She really didn't need a new round of drama, she thought.

'All right, the kids are here with me and we can leave right away. I'll have to go to the main house and ask to borrow Pete's car.'

'Good idea,' said Jed. 'But hurry, please. I don't want anything to happen to you. You're so precious to me.'

Jenny, warmed by these words, had no time to reply. She hung up, grabbed the kids and a few belongings, her purse and mobile. Then she set off across the paddock to the main house.

Fortunately the kids could see she was in a hurry and ran with her. They really liked to visit the big house, as there were always fresh-baked cakes and biscuits to be had.

As Jenny approached the house she glanced around. There was plenty of cleared ground all the way to the drive and the main road beyond. She couldn't see any vehicles approaching.

Liz came out of the house as she approached. 'Hello Jenny, nice to see you and the kids.'

She bent down to the children and said quietly, 'There's a new batch of rock cakes sitting on the kitchen table if you want one or two.'

She lifted her eyebrows as she spoke and the kids rushed off with a squeal.

Jenny spoke quietly to Liz.

'John has found where we are by the emails sent from Jed and us. Jed thinks John's on his way here, and he's had plenty of time, all day, to get here. He might even be here now.'

They both looked around towards the road.

'I need to leave. Jed suggested that I move into a motel in town, and then catch the next train back to his property. Can I borrow your car to get into town? Perhaps one of the men could pick it up tomorrow.'

'Of course, Jenny. Whatever you need. We'll do whatever you want,' Liz reassured her.

'I'd appreciate it if you don't tell John that we've just left or he'll rush back into town to find us.'

They walked towards the house, where Liz found the keys to the second car while Jenny called the children. They came running with their mouths full of rock cake and an extra one in each hand.

Jenny squatted down to be on a level with their eyes.

'Jed has just phoned and wants us to come home to him straight away. So we're going now. I want you to get into the car. I have brought teddy and big dog with me so they won't be left behind. Now off we go.'

The children grabbed their toys and ran to the car. Once in, they were buckled into their seat belts and then bounced up and down, waiting to start. They were already talking about things they might do with Jed when they got there.

Jenny started the motor and set off down the drive. She hoped that John wouldn't be coming up from the opposite direction as there was no other way out.

She reached the main road safely and turned towards town. There were quite a number of cars and trucks on the road, so she felt John would not see her or the children.

In Morwell there were two motels and a pub. She stopped at the motel closest to the railway station, as they would need to walk there for the first train in the morning. She hadn't been in Morwell long enough to be known by the motel people but she didn't have any trouble getting a family room with few questions asked. She phoned for a pizza to be delivered to their room so they wouldn't have to go out and risk bumping into John.

The children spent their time looking at the little soaps and biscuits available in the room, before settling in to watch kids' TV programs. Jenny made a cup of tea to quieten her nerves. She then rang down to reception to see when the next train left. It was the mail train at 6am and it would go straight through to Melbourne and then all stations beyond that to Port Fairy.

She began to relax. They'd made it before John could discover where they were. She prayed they would again.

Chapter 39

Am I obsessed or even possessed? Am I like John?

I rationalised that I was not hurting anyone.

Had it taken me just two weeks to become so mad? After the fire, then the men at the beach walkway and, finally, John at our door threatening us, I'd had enough. On top of all that, Jenny had phoned to tell us about the fast exit she'd had to make from Morwell back to Jed's place after John had uncovered their whereabouts. It was all too much. I wanted to find him and confront him on my terms.

I didn't want to be like the person I had become since he'd been threatening us, someone who cowered and was scared.

I was ready to threaten him instead. I wanted to keep the pressure on him and see how he liked it.

There I was in bed, thinking all this through again, desperate for a sleep-in, but early morning sounds kept intruding on me.

Next door a lawnmower was spluttering noisily near the fence. Children were walking along the footpath across the road, hitting fence palings intermittently with a stick. The chatter of their voices was broken every now and then with a shriek of laughter. The day had begun.

I'd struck some good luck with Margaret from creative writing class, who lived in the next street, selling her house and a second car, so she could move into a smaller unit. Downsizing, she called it. I'd noticed the 'for sale' sign on the back window of the car when Mac and I were out walking. That car was just what I wanted to find John.

It was a small grey Yaris in need of a paint job and with a few dings on each side. Margaret explained that it had originally belonged to her niece who had now gone overseas and she wanted the money from its sale to further her travels. Because of its poor condition, it was at a price I was prepared to pay, which was almost nothing.

I chatted for a while with Margaret after signing the papers. I was now the proud owner of a third car. But I didn't take it home with pride. I drove it to the street behind our street and next to a footpath that cut through from our street. I didn't want anyone to associate this car with us. It was only intended for use in finding John. I was going to discover where he lived and accost him. I would be assertive, or maybe even aggressive.

I would advise him that we would talk to the police if he kept up his harassment. On many occasions when I couldn't sleep I'd imagined whole conversations where I would have my say and John would eventually apologise and stop his antics.

I just needed to find him. I knew that I would see John's Mazda at some time in our street and when I did, I would be able to follow him home. I had already tried to use the internet directory to find him but had had no luck, goodness knows why. So now I was going to find him another way.

I told Mac what I'd done. He thought it was a bad plan, and dangerous. That I was behaving badly. He wouldn't be part of it. But perhaps because he also thought it was a crazy plan that I'd never have the courage to pull off, he humoured me.

'What are you going to do when you find out where he lives?' he asked.

I just shrugged my shoulders and couldn't answer.

Within a week I'd seen the blue Mazda and followed it. I had come out to the letterbox and noticed the car sitting on the street several doors up from us. I quickly dropped the letters onto the hall table and walked out the back, taking my keys with me. I called out to Mac that I was going to the shop and I wouldn't be long.

Then I rushed along the footpath and hopped in my new-old car. Luckily it started immediately, so I did a U-turn and came out onto our street about two hundred metres from where the Mazda was sitting facing the other way. I stopped, turned off the motor and sat there ready to wait.

I was a bit worried that if the Mazda stayed parked for a long time, Mac would be concerned, thinking that I hadn't returned from the shops. But it was only a few minutes before its engine started up and it pulled out from the kerb.

I followed.

To my surprise I was able to stay two cars back without John seeming to notice me. Before long he turned into Pittwater Road and stayed on it until he reached Narrabeen. Soon he slowed down to curve into the lake carpark and stopped. I stopped before reaching the entrance and hovered there until he'd beeped his car lock. He walked swiftly to a house next to the parking area and bounded up its steps, before I too parked at the other end of the parking area.

The house was an old beach-style wooden cottage that fronted Pittwater Road and backed onto a track looking out onto Narrabeen Lake. I was astonished that, if this was his place, he only lived five kilometres from our old home.

As he first bent over the letterbox and then searched for his house keys, I took stock of his appearance. His crumpled suit, a navy pin stripe, hung on his frame as if he'd slept in it. His hair stood up in peaks and his face looked unshaven. As he'd raced up the steps he'd knocked the letterbox and bumped into a post at the front door. *Had he been drinking again in the middle of the day?*

When he was safely inside, I got out of the car and walked down the track between the properties and the lake. At this time of day, there were plenty of kids on bikes zipping to and fro and parents with strollers. Ducks waddled around as if they owned the land. Some were native ducks and some were hybrids that had crossed with white domestic ducks. Many of the hybrids looked very ugly and I despaired about this, as the council had tried to rid the area of domestic ducks to maintain the purity of the wild ducks.

All of them were tame and came running when they heard the rustling of paper or the popping of sandwich boxes.

John's house was the only one that backed onto the track with a fence and back entrance gate. All the other properties were shops that filled the grounds with storage sheds at the back and had no gardens or fences.

I walked back to the car and drove home, leaving it where I'd parked it in the street next to ours.

'Guess what?' I said, coming into the house. 'I know where John lives and you wouldn't believe it, it's just at Narrabeen.'

Mac looked at me. 'You're asking for trouble. I don't want to know and neither should you.'

But I couldn't seem to give it up. I chose times when Mac was having a nap or at bowls for the chance to drive over to John's house again.

Sometimes I saw John at his place and stayed hidden in the car, although I didn't really need to as I always came prepared with a heavy coat or shirt and hat as a disguise. Sometimes I just walked past the fence along the track, and if the coast was clear I would look over the gate into his backyard.

That was when I began to feel that I'd become obsessed or possessed.

What am I doing? Why do I need to be here? If I'm not going to accost him as I've been planning, then what am I doing?

I was debating this question with myself when I suddenly came upon the answer. It had been lingering at the back of my brain, in a small insignificant corner so that I wouldn't notice it. I guess it was such a big and frightful thing to think, that I must have been trying to ignore it.

I wanted to kill John!

Chapter 40

That night I couldn't sleep. Why am I thinking about killing someone, I kept thinking?

I was a normal person who hated war and criminal activity. The only time I used the word 'kill' was when I said things like, 'This headache is killing me' or 'I'd kill for some chocolate cake'. It was never real. These were only things that you said. Just expressions. But here I was thinking about it for real.

I felt as if I had come to the end of the road. Jenny and Mac and I had weathered many terrible things. No one was happy. No one was safe. Mac was not well. It was taking a toll on him. We had lost most of what we'd owned: our house, our money and our peace of mind. I couldn't get rid of the thought that I could kill John and all our troubles would be over. This idea crept into my mind and wouldn't leave.

It was like a fog that you don't see at first, just wisps of air that begin to whirl around you. Then you blink and find that you're immersed in the fog. It's all around you, seeping into all the corners of your sight and your mind, until you're not able to see anything in front or behind you, just white blank air that you breathe and taste and know you want.

I knew Mac would be horrified. I would be horrified too if I was still the ordinary me: wife, mother, grandmother, neighbour and friend.

But I was not ordinary me. I was a person with a mission, a purpose. I was going to save my family. No one else could do it, not the police, just me. I was the only one who had the gumption to take what had been dealt out to me, and run with it no matter what the consequences. I felt a bit like a lioness protecting her cubs from danger.

I knew how others who had gone before me had felt. Women who had killed their abusive husbands after being beaten for ten years or a mother who discovered an uncle had been sexually abusing her 12-year-old for five years. Women who were angry and rightly so. Angry beyond all understanding by others. Now I had an insight into how they must have felt, because I was feeling that same amount of anger. Even while I also felt helpless and hopeless. I was full of hate.

I tried not to think about killing John, and at first I could keep busy with housework in our rented place, and working in the garden, and I took walks with Mac. But eventually the obsession took over my mind and I could think of nothing else. I looked up books about death; I googled 'murder' on the internet without even thinking of the consequences of leaving cyber clues for police; I read comments on the subject of murder on random blogs; I read about famous crimes; I even began to read the labels on poisons in the supermarket.

I listed in my mind all the ways one could kill a person. But I never wrote anything down. I kept my thoughts a secret.

Then I googled ways to kill, researching one method at a time, thinking about how easily I could accomplish a murder, and how I would feel doing it. The list I made in my head contained six methods, all tried and true in every crime novel I'd ever read. They were shooting, stabbing, choking, hanging, hitting someone over the head and poisoning.

I researched all of them. Thank goodness for Wikipedia, I thought.

Shooting: 'The degree of tissue disruption caused by a projectile such as a bullet causes a permanent cavity as it passes through, resulting in ballistic trauma.'

Bullets left blood-splatter and there was a problem if you missed a vital organ such as the brain or heart. The biggest problem, of course, was that I'd never handled a gun, I didn't know how to buy one, and I didn't think I would be accurate because I could hardly throw a ball through a hoop in a basketball game. So how would I be with a person as a target?

Stabbing: 'In a close encounter a knife can be more fatal than a gun.' Stabbings happened often on the street. But if the target moved or retaliated, those stabbings were usually not fatal, in fact they were often not significant.'

Of course I didn't want any close encounter. I imagined trying to stab John. I would raise the knife, he would grab my arm, twist it behind me, take the knife and stab me instead. I would have no strength against a stronger and younger man.

Choking: 'Most choking deaths are age-related. It was reported that Attila the Hun choked to death with the aid of his wife.'

The act of compressing someone's neck or strangling was a common method. I found one case of a girl strangled with pantyhose. I didn't have any pantyhose. I wondered what I could use. A rope seemed too thick. I knew I could never pull the knots tight enough and a wire used like a garrotte would cut the neck and almost take the head off. Ugh. I felt nauseous as I pictured the scene.

Hanging: 'Hanging is the lethal suspension of a person by a ligature.'

How could I get John to stand still on a chair and hang himself? Because I'd never have the strength to lift an unconscious person up into a noose and pull it. So that was out.

Hitting someone over the head: Hitting someone over the head when they were not looking might have been a possibility for me, but how could I creep up behind John without him noticing? Even if I could, how could I wield a big enough blow from the angle of a 1.6 metre-high person to a 1.8 metre-high person, so that it would kill him?

Poisoning: This seemed the most likely possibility. Many famous persons had been poisoned with a variety of poisons such as hemlock, chloride, cyanide, arsenic, domestic liquids and even plants such as poisonous mushrooms, rhubarb leaves and oleander branches.

I recalled a story about a group of scouts on a bush camp, who had cooked their meal by threading oleander sticks through their sausages and holding them over the camp fire. The oleander poison had seeped into the sausages, and on eating them the boys 'upped and died'. I didn't know if this was a true story or not but there was no way I could get John to eat a plate of poisonous mushrooms, presuming I knew how to find them, or a sausage or two cooked on oleander sticks or even a dish of rhubarb leaves sprinkled on ice cream.

There had also been stories of people being fed arsenic in their Weetbix every morning for two to three months until they died. I read that this method masked the poison so the police and doctors thought the victims had simply been ill and died.

A new method of poisoning I'd read about in novels – because most of my information came from novels – was an injection of poison into a tube of toothpaste. The victim died as soon as he or she brushed their teeth. More fool them for wanting to have a winning smile.

All these methods really required a person to be living in the home of the person they were trying to eradicate. So that left me out. Besides, all the stories about poisoning also talked about the agony a person would go through before dying.

I hated John, but I didn't want him to suffer to that degree. That would be cruel, I thought. In my obsessed foggy state I couldn't see that killing someone was in itself as cruel as one could ever get. Finally, I recognised that I couldn't do it. Not any of it. I couldn't kill a person no matter how much I hated them.

I had little knowledge of how to carry out any of those lethal acts, and I had no skills whatsoever.

Also my fear of being caught remained there in the back of my foggy mind. I had always disliked stories or movies about people in jail. I had a very vivid imagination and could picture the agony of being in a little cell with nothing to do for years on end. I could also picture from films I'd seen, the other, perhaps brutish, people I might have to deal with in jail. It filled me with horror.

Every now and then the fog would lift and I would see myself in prison forever. But mostly the fog was overwhelming in my mind and I could see nothing but how to get rid of John. I realise now that the way the subject of murder had at times completely taken over my mind seems laughable, but when I was caught up in the fog it was deadly serious.

I was just a step away from becoming a murderer.

Chapter 41

My obsessive drive to the Narrabeen Lakes carpark became a habit that continued for weeks.

But one night, after I'd arrived and was sitting in my car, the fog began to lift and all at once my mind became sharp and clear.

It all now seemed like a figment of my imagination. The past few weeks seemed like a dream. It was as if I'd been in therapy. Therapy that would create preposterous scenarios, draw on my imaginative fantasies, and extend my usual moral code beyond recognition. All this in order to flush the anger out of my feverish mind and bring me back to normality.

I had taken my usual trip along Pittwater Road to the lake carpark while Mac was in bed asleep. He was perpetually tired and not well, while I was strung out and couldn't sleep until about 1am, and even then I only napped for a few hours at a time.

The dark hours were often when I would sneak out of the house and drive to John's place. This particular night, I slid out of the car and walked along the lakeside track as I always did. It was a pattern of behaviour that I was following, ingrained in me since my obsession had begun – to walk the pathway to the fence and look over his gate.

There was no one around as it was after ten o'clock at night. The moon was partly behind a few scudding clouds but still brightened the trees and the track. Water lapped at the mangroves near the bank of the lake and silver streaks of moonlight speared out into the middle of the water.

I had just come to the decision that I would not do this anymore.

'I will sell the car and never come near this place again,' I whispered to myself as I leant on the gate.

I was making a New Year's resolution, a bit late, but more resolute than any I had made before, when a man and woman came hurrying along the path, holding onto each other's waists and whispering to each other.

They were about twenty-five to thirty years old and were wearing casual summer clothes. They'd probably had dinner at one of the restaurants further along the lakeside track overlooking the water. They were really only interested in each other until they noticed me. Then they slowed down and stared.

For a second, I felt as if I was looking down at myself and seeing the scene from their perspective. I looked like a thief. They had a good view of me. I hadn't worn my hat as it was so hot and dark. I knew they would be able to say I was 1.6 metres tall, with brown hair, white skin, and aged about 50. They could even contact the police as soon as they were around the corner and out of sight.

I had to make a decision quickly.

A wave and a nod to them, a quick good evening and an entry via the gate, which fortunately was not locked, seemed natural. I shut it after me and leant on the panels of wood. I could hear the couple's slow footsteps and giggly whispers as they scuttled off. I had fooled them.

Great!

Now I was in the backyard of the property, the one I had decided to never come near again. The yard was small, with no plants, just bare grass that looked as if it hadn't been mown or watered for some time. There was a verandah across the back of the house that could be reached by two concrete steps. There was just one wrought iron chair on the verandah with a number of empty beer bottles beside it on the floor. The house was in darkness and I could hear no sounds at all.

I was just about to turn around and go back out the way I had come in, when I heard scrabbling noises at the gate. Someone was coming in. It could only be John.

I took the three steps back to the verandah hoping to hide, but there was nowhere to go except into the house via the back door which was slightly open. He must have just ducked out for something and was now coming back.

I stepped through the door and quietly closed it, holding the handle until I felt it touch the wooden frame before letting it go, so there would be no click. I hoped I had been fast enough so John hadn't seen it close. The house was in deep darkness. I fumbled along a hall with my hands stretched out on both sides to touch the walls.

All the time I was listening for John's footsteps on the path and up the stairs. A sliding noise told me he had reached the wooden verandah floor.

My left hand felt the shape of a door. I ran my hand down the wood until I touched a handle and pulled. I felt inside. It seemed like a broom cupboard. I stepped in and pulled it shut behind me, just as the back door was opened and then slammed back shut.

John was home!

He was in the hallway, muttering a few curses to himself. I could imagine the annoyance that would be on his face at this moment and how it would change to real anger if he saw me. I couldn't trust myself to breathe. But holding my breath was getting too hard. I let out my breath as quietly as I could and then breathed slowly through my mouth.

I had heard that people could sense when someone was nearby. Some change in the atmosphere or something technical like that. I had certainly felt it when I had been alone in the house while Mac was in hospital, and in that instance there was no one there. It was just my imagination. So the presence would surely be much stronger if someone was actually in the house.

John didn't turn on any light, which was comforting. He just stumbled down the hall and I could hear him bumping into the wall at several spots. It came to me then that he was drunk.

Perhaps he would get into bed and go straight to sleep, so then I could creep out. I crossed my fingers. I desperately wanted something to go right for me now, especially as I had just made up my mind never to do this again.

Chapter 42

I dared not move – not wanting brooms or whatever else was in the cupboard to come crashing down.

John continued to bump into the hallway walls as he stumbled past me to the front of the house. I heard a door open, the sound of a few steps, then a loud creak that sounded as if he had thrown himself onto the bed. I pictured the shape of the house in my mind. It was an old cottage, small, with both front and back doors on the same side.

I thought it was probably typical of the fifties, with a hall down one side and doors leading off it to a front bedroom, a second bedroom, a lounge/dining area, a kitchen and bathroom with a laundry at the back. I was probably in the broom cupboard between the bathroom and the kitchen.

I thought about what I'd heard. Judging by the sound of his footsteps and banging around, John was probably drunk again. He was no doubt now in the front bedroom, taking off his coat. He might then come down the hall to the bathroom or the kitchen. I would have to stay where I was and hope that he wouldn't want to use a broom at 10 o'clock at night.

I couldn't risk finding my way to the back door and having John switch on the hall light just at the moment I was at the door. So I stayed where I was. There was no time to consider what I'd done, only time to think about how to get away.

I heard him coming down the hallway again. I could tell he'd gone into the next room which was probably the second bedroom and now he was turning on the computer. The little trill of the computer warming up told me this.

I heard more footsteps in the hall, a shuffle and bang, and then a muttered curse, then another light clicked. Was it the bathroom or the kitchen?

A clink of glass on glass told me he had poured a drink. The light clicked off before another light clicked on. This could be the bathroom. The sound of water running set my mind racing. Perhaps I could get out while he was washing his face or hands. Then I heard shoes being flung off and hitting the floor and the slosh of water being dispersed.

He was in the bath. I was nearly sure but didn't want to move too soon.

I heard more sloshing water and a sigh, and then a clink, possibly as a glass was put down on the side of the bath. Yes, I was almost sure he was settled in the bath and I could escape.

Quietly I opened the door a crack or two then I slid out, holding my breath when a broom handle tilted towards me. I grabbed it and placed it back in position.

I could see now by the light from the bathroom door, which was slightly open. I was glad that it opened away from me so that I was not immediately exposed in the doorway.

Without thinking, I peeped through the crack made by the space between the frame and the open door. I could see John through a misty fug of steam. He was up to his neck in water with the taps still running and was in jeopardy of having the water run over the edge and on to the floor. I could see the full whisky glass that he had placed on the bath edge next to his head as he leant back against the rim, and the nearly full bottle of whiskey on the floor nearby. I even noticed it was *Jack Daniels Black Label.* Thank goodness his eyes were closed.

He gave a snore that startled me and then when he sank down into the tub I worried that my luck was up. He was sure to wake up when his nose touched the water. It was time to get out. If I waited a second more he would be awake, for sure, and he'd pull himself up out of the water and see me.

I tiptoed to the back door, opened it quietly and stepped out onto the verandah. I softly snicked the door behind me and ran quietly down the steps to the gate, suddenly afraid that he was behind me and I would be caught at the last minute.

I peeped out as I opened the gate, ready to look as if I belonged there, but no one was on the track. I hurried to the carpark. There were still a few cars there. Probably locals who had no room in their garages for their second car. It made my car less noticeable.

It wasn't until I was home in bed next to Mac, who hadn't stirred when I'd sneaked back in, that the full horror of my night escapade hit me.

I considered the bad luck of my timing. I had just decided never to go there again when I was caught inside. But my good luck in getting out of the house when I did was amazing. My bed had never seemed so cosy and safe.

But the adrenalin in my body was so high that I lay awake for a couple of hours before I could begin to relax. Then I slept.

The next day I told Mac I was selling the car.

'So you aren't going to hover around John's house anymore?' Mac asked.

'No, never again,' I said firmly.

I drove the car to a sales yard with Mac following in our family car. The salesperson offered only the minimum of $300 for the car. I knew it was a rip off, but was just so glad to be rid of it, that I accepted.

The rest of the day was quiet. Mac listened to some classical CDs while I read a Marian Keyes novel. I began to think my life was all a dream.

At about 2am that night I heard a noise. I opened my eyes and there was John. His hands were outstretched towards my throat. He spat at me with a twisted face. *Why were you in my house hiding in the broom cupboard? What were you going to do? Did you try to poison me with whisky and rat poison? Would you have liked to see me foaming at the mouth and twisting in pain? The rope and the gun wouldn't work, would it? Why don't you try it now?* He looped the noose over my head and pulled it tight around my neck.

My hands clawed at my neck as it became harder and harder for me to breathe.

Perhaps the knife would be better, whispered John, lunging forward so that a knife he was holding cut into my arm. He stabbed the knife down into the pillow near my head. Suddenly a gun in his right hand pressed hard against the middle of my forehead. He bared his teeth in the semblance of a smile and I heard him pull the trigger.

I screamed and flung myself over Mac who reflexively jumped up into a sitting position.

'I'm shot. I'm dying,' I yelled.

Mac shook me. 'Wake up, Lilli. It's just a nightmare.'

I looked around me. No blood on my pyjamas or on the bed linen. No hole in my forehead and no John with a rope and a knife.

'What was that about?' Mack looked shaky himself.

'I don't know. Just a nightmare, I guess. I'm just so overwrought. It must all be catching up with me.'

Mac pulled me down so my head was on his chest.

'I suppose you've been obsessed with John for so long he's inhabiting your dreams now.'

'I know, I know. But no more, that was it. I feel so much better now.'

For a few moments there, the dream had seemed so real.

I rolled back over onto my side of the bed, feeling grateful that it wasn't real after all.

For a second time I felt lucky to be alive.

Chapter 43

Two days later, I was still in a fragile state.

We slept late. Then a loud knock on the door woke us. It sounded just like the last time the police had called by, when Sid, the identity thief, had been murdered.

I got out of bed cautiously, cinched in my dressing gown, and shuffled behind Mac to the front door.

When I saw two bulky, fit young policemen I nearly collapsed. Had they discovered I'd been in John's house and had come to take me away?

'May we come in?' one said.

'Show me your badge,' Mac said. He examined it. After introductions and an invitation to come in, we sat on the lounge looking expectantly at them. The tallest of the two began.

'We are here because your daughter, Ms Jenny Stanford, is the next of kin to your son-in-law.'

'What about Jenny?' A rising panic sounded in my voice.

'There's nothing wrong with your daughter. We just don't know where she is and we have some bad news for her.'

'What's happened?' Mac enquired. 'Can you tell us? Jenny, our daughter, is in Victoria and only has a mobile.'

'I'm afraid your son-in-law has had an accident.'

'An accident! Is he okay?' Mac queried.

'Normally we would be advising the next of kin first but as she hasn't been contactable, you're our next option. Unfortunately we have some bad news, John Stanford is dead.'

John! Dead!

My mind tried to take it in. I had wanted this for a long time. Now it had happened and I couldn't believe it. Mac and I just sat still, gazing at them.

The police were quite taken aback. I think they expected us to show some concern or sadness but we showed none.

'What happened?' My voice shook a little.

'A neighbour of Mr Stanford saw water pouring out of a break in the wall at the side of the house. He knocked on the door and when there was no answer, he called us. We discovered Mr. Stanford in the bath. He had drowned. We are sorry for his loss to you and your daughter.'

I clasped my throat. I was remembering John asleep in the bath through the crack in the door.

Mac, who had none of those memories asked, 'When did this happen and how could he drown?'

'The doctor who attended the death reported that he had imbibed a large amount of alcohol, about triple the legal limit for driving. We think he must have fallen asleep in the bath and drowned.

'When was this?' Mac asked.

'We've calculated that it was about two days ago.'

'Will there be an investigation into his death?'

'There usually is when a death is unexplained. But the doctor, who is also the local coroner, has said that it's a straightforward case – unless other evidence comes to light.'

'Thank you,' said Mac. 'Our daughter has a prepaid mobile phone but it's often not on. We'll try to reach her as soon as we can so she can contact you. We still have the number for the local station.'

'Right.' The tall policeman stood up and turned towards the door. 'Let us know as soon as you have contacted Ms Stanford, as we need to discuss the procedures for claiming the body.'

They moved to the door, nodding their goodbyes. The tall one turned at the last moment and said, 'I notice that you don't seem to be very upset about your son-in-law's death. Is there a reason?'

'Our son-in-law was not a good husband to Jenny and she had left him,' Mac answered. 'So we haven't been inclined to see him favourably. Of course we're sad that he's died, just as we would be sad that anyone we knew had died. We are also sad that the children's father has died. But, no, we are not as unhappy as we would normally be about a family member.'

The policeman nodded thoughtfully at this, said goodbye again and strode to his car. I wondered what he was thinking about us.

I collapsed on the lounge. Two days ago was when I was there. I'd probably seen him just before he drowned.

'Were you there near the house the other night,' Mac asked me softly.

I nodded unhappily. 'If it happened on Tuesday night, I was there. I was there near the house, just like I have been all the other times, but I didn't see him die, or know that he was dead.'

I looked squarely at Mac. I couldn't tell him I had been inside the house. He only knew that I went by the house. I fudged it a little. I was telling the truth even if it wasn't all the truth, and he believed me. I knew I was concealing the whole story, but what good would it do to say where I was hiding?

Mac was in reflective mood.

'I remember the woman at the Opera House said he had been drinking a lot and that was one reason why they fired him, and why she rejected him.'

I nodded. I still found it hard to talk.

'This is fortuitous. *Karma*, if you like. What comes around goes around, as the saying goes. I can't pretend to be really upset about it. Just upset for Jenny. After all she married him in love and didn't expect things to end this way.

'Let's try to ring her now,' I said.

'You know … this is not the way to tell her. We need to see her. She'll be sad no matter what has happened in the past and the children will be very upset. Don't forget they have lots of good memories as well as bad. I'll ring Jed now and tell him the situation and ask him to break it to her. I'll also tell him we'll be there as soon as we can.'

I sat on the bed. I couldn't think or do anything.

I was there such a long while that Mac came to find me.

'Was it my fault? I wished him dead,' I whispered fearfully.

'Never,' said Mac. 'He was an intelligent adult who made some bad choices in his life. He fell asleep in the bath after drinking too much. Everyone is responsible for their own actions.

I thought about this and said to myself, *Only if no one is there to help.*

I hugged Mac. He was always so supportive and sensible.

But how could I make sense of my actions? Maybe I should have woken John that night? Or was he so drunk he wouldn't have stirred? Did it happen at the time I was there or was it another bath time? I was kidding myself, of course.

Eventually I came to understand that it would have happened even if I hadn't been there, and the consequences of any action on my part would have been disastrous. At last my mind began to accept Mac's words. It wasn't my fault.

I felt the bubbles of relief begin in my stomach. They filled my chest and moved up to my brain. I was light-headed. I could see the bubbles in multi-colours of lemon, aqua and pink just like ice-cream colours. They drifted and floated through the top of my head and spread all around me, bumping me softly and popping quietly. I felt new.

All the worries I'd accumulated and had been tamping down inside me for so long were enclosed in those bubbles and were being sent up in the air and away. Even the bubbles holding tiny pieces of guilt. I began to feel wonderful.

Then I stopped myself. A man had died. A man who was the father of our grandchildren. Why couldn't I feel some pity? I didn't know. All I knew was that I was happy.

A parcel of positive thoughts crept into my head. *Jenny can marry Jed now and be happy again on a farm in Victoria. The kids will remember their father, but have a new person who they will grow to love and who already loves them. Tony and Samantha will either stay in Brisbane or come back to Sydney. It will be their choice, not thrust upon them. Mac will feel better as his blood pressure lowers without any stress in his life. We'll build a new home to make more good memories.*

And I ...?

Although there's a tinge of guilt that will remain with me forever, I'm prepared to live with that.

I will be free of fears and cares.

Chapter 44

Detective Rogers turned to the McGregor file as he prepared to speak. A meeting was being held in the police station's small conference room around midday.

Officers Sgt Ronson, Constable Bailey and Detective Hughes were there with their notebooks and pens, chatting away until the meeting began.

'There have been a number of occasions where we have been called by the McGregors regarding concerns over their son-in-law. If the Coroner rules that the death of John Stanford is not accidental, we'll need to follow this up.'

Rogers walked over to the whiteboard. 'Of course the death could be accidental, suicide or murder.'

Ronson spoke up. 'The first time we interviewed the McGregors was over the death of a man known for fraud crimes. He had their names and address in his pocket. If that's not suspicious, I don't know what is.'

Bailey broke in with a different view.

'I don't think that has anything to do with Stanford's death though. Although it remains a possibility that they may have mixed with enough criminals to pay someone to kill Stanford for them.'

'Let's add that to our investigation, but not make a decision yet,' Rogers said. 'The next incidents were broken windows, a nasty blog, a violent attack by some thugs and a fire. They accused Stanford each time.'

At this point Hughes decided he should join in the conversation.

'They told me they were being stalked and they thought it was Stanford. Now Stanford is dead. That's a motive. Maybe they were so angry that they went to see him and killed him in a rage?'

'Let's consider this may be a murder and do some initial investigation before we hear from the Coroner,' Detective Rogers suggested. 'Ronson, will you look into the whereabouts of the McGregors, and their daughter, Jenny Stanford, at the time of Stanford's death? Bailey, get me some information about their jobs, hobbies, etcetera. I'll phone the fire chief for more about the fire and also talk to the Sydney City Central police about Sol Harmon's death. Aside from this, keep the investigation centred on John Stanford: his whereabouts, his state of mind, and his actions on the day he died. It may just be an accident or suicide. We won't know until we receive the report.'

The next morning at 9 o'clock, they met again. Most of the group looked bleary-eyed from a night of investigation. Cups of coffee steamed on the table, which was strewn with papers, notebooks and breakfast crumbs.

Rogers nodded to Bailey, who supplied what information she'd gleaned.

'Mr McGregor was a teacher, now retired. He plays bowls twice a week and is at home most other days. His wife was a teacher too, also retired and her weekly activities are more creative. Neighbours from their previous home, before the fire, tell me they were well-respected, and they were very upset when their daughter went missing last year. They didn't alert us about that. I wonder why not?'

Ronson spoke up. 'It seems that Stanford blamed them for her disappearance and they were frightened of him. Maybe they were right. Regardless, both were at home on the night in question. No one saw them go out, either walking or by any form of transport. Sydney City Central police said they thought the McGregors' stories were flimsy as to why they were in the pub where Sol Harmon was killed, but there's now been an arrest of a well-known member of a gang for that crime. The McGregors phoned with their daughter's address and phone number and advised they were going to visit her tomorrow. They may be away for a few weeks.'

Rogers tapped his pen on his teeth.

'I think I'll arrange an interview before they leave. Just to be sure.'

He stood up, collecting his notebook and files from the table. Everyone else did the same and then disappeared into the main office to continue their reports.

....

Mac opened his door and escorted the police officers into his lounge room, as if it was a regular routine by now. Detective Rogers, with Sgt Ronson and Constable Bailey.

Sgt Ronson cleared his throat.

'We have noted that you have made a number of complaints about your son-in-law and that it was suspected that he had set fire to your home. Mr McGregor, you have also had harassment from a blog that has come to our attention. It seems that you would have a motive and opportunity to harm John Stanford. What do you say to these allegations?

I cringed. I was certain they were going to take me away.

They must have viewed us as suspects in John's death and investigated us, I thought. The file in their office obviously showed that we were frightened of, and angry at, John. We might be at the top of their suspects list. Especially me.

I began to shake. I could see myself in prison. In a small room with no comforts and without Mac. I began to have a panic attack. My breathing became raspy and I struggled to get enough air into my lungs. Mac turned to me and noticed that I was gulping and holding my hand to my throat.

In an instant, he became very angry.

'How dare you!' he said. 'My wife is so upset by this. You think we might have harmed John and that he was not the cause of his own death? As if we are the type of people who would do something like that? We did see him at the fire and we have been harassed but we would never kill him.'

They looked at me, a bit bashful now that Mac had pointed out my distress, waiting, I suppose, for my agreement with what Mac had said. I took a big strained breath, gulped, and said in a very small voice which was all that could come out of my mouth, 'I don't even know when he died'.

The police looked strangely at me.

'I mean how could we have done anything, I don't even know

when it happened,' Mac said, sounding even more innocent than I did, and I thought they could hear that innocence.

The tallest policeman examined his notes.

'He died on Tuesday evening between 10pm and 3am in the early morning of Wednesday.'

My befuddled mind raced back to Tuesday. *Was it Tuesday that I went around there? Yes, it was Tuesday. So he did die on Tuesday night or were they saying Wednesday?*

Fortunately Mac was also unsure about what they were saying.

'Do you mean Tuesday evening or Wednesday evening?'

'Sometime Tuesday evening or Wednesday early morning,' Rogers said. 'Evidently he went to see about a job on Tuesday and seemed to be drinking and taking drugs in the afternoon and evening. He must have had a bath about 10pm and stayed there until he drowned.'

I was horrified.

It was me. I was there Tuesday evening, late, perhaps almost Wednesday early. I tried to contain my horror and hoped the police would see it as grief that my son-in-law was dead. I didn't want them to interpret my body language differently.

'We need to formally interview you tomorrow before you leave for Victoria. A police car will pick you up at 8.30am.'

I was feeling so worried and so was Mac, but for a different reason. He sat me down with a cup of tea and tried to make me relax.

Then he spoke very quietly, looking directly at me.

'What if they conclude that we had a motive for this and his death becomes a murder case?'

I covered my face with my hands in agony. Motives were the key to deciding if a person was guilty or not. There had been plenty of instances in books and in the papers over the years of people who had been wrongly accused, and had spent years in jail until they were finally able to prove their innocence. It would be my fate to find myself accused of doing the wrong thing, when in fact I hadn't really done anything.

………………..

We were back in the police station again. If the first time was frightening, this time was so harrowing I couldn't stop shaking.

'For the record, I'm Detective Rogers and you are here to formally answer some questions about Mr John Stanford.'

'Should we have a lawyer with us?' Mac asked.

'It's not necessary just yet. These are just preliminary questions about the issues you have encountered.'

For the next hour and a half we retold the stories about each incident he mentioned from a file in front of him. Eventually he put his concerns to us bluntly.

'It seems that John Stanford was disliked by both of you and was causing a great deal of trouble. Did you kill him? Did you find an opportunity to get rid of him so your daughter and you would be spared his stalking and harassment?'

Both Mac and I were shocked by these questions. Should we be saying anything or should we now ask for a lawyer? Would it be better to just give honest answers? After all, we were innocent. I didn't know what to do.

Detective Rogers sat patiently waiting for an answer.

Mac took the lead. 'We have nothing to do with John's death. I didn't like him because he was abusive to our daughter, but I could never kill anyone, and I have never been to John's home.'

I wanted to say the same but I would have to lie. 'Me too,' I said as confidently as I could.

That was the answer Rogers wants. I bet he can most often tell when people are lying.

Constable Bailey eventually led us to the station doors. As they swung closed behind us, a great sense of relief swept over me.

Mac was angry. 'How dare they think one of us, or both of us, might kill John? This is too much.'

I nodded but I couldn't say anything. I'd been there. I might be the reason John died. I had lied to the police and I still felt guilty.

Chapter 45

The police interview was such a shock.

To think that the police suspected that either one or both of us could have killed John. The idea matched those deep, deep thoughts I already had. I was guilty. It was all very well to believe I was not, but the police suspected us. Well, suspected me.

Will the police discover I was there in the house? What do they do to investigate a death?

I now knew that an unnatural death is investigated with an autopsy. If it was decided that a crime had been committed, would police be looking for finger prints? I had left mine on the back door and the broom cupboard.

Would they be asking locals if they'd seen a strange person near the property? The canoodling couple on the lake walkway would be able to identify me.

I became so frightened I couldn't move or speak to anyone.

Mac wondered what was wrong with me.

I couldn't tell him.

'Surely, you're not so sad about John?' he asked me.

I just shook my head.

I needed to get away. Thank goodness we were driving down to Victoria tomorrow. The drive would be pleasant and take our minds off our worries. Seeing Jenny and the children again would do me the most good too.

Bags packed and in the car, we were almost off.

The last task was to ask Jean if she would collect our mail. Although we had moved a few streets away after the fire, we hoped that she'd be able to do this for us. Jean agreed with a smile and I thanked her profusely. We gave her our address and phone contact in case she needed us, before we set off with a wave.

The highway took us past Yass and down to Albury. Then we branched off to Port Fairy, which was a small village on the south coast of Victoria, part of the spectacular shipwreck coast region, and very picturesque. My worries eased as I took in the view.

Jed lived about fifty kilometres inland from there and it didn't take us long to find his property.

We phoned Jenny when we were near, so she, Chiara and Ryan were waiting outside on the verandah. The children ran down to the car and I leapt out to give them big hugs. Just to have their small bodies warm and close was wonderful.

Jed had joined Jenny on the verandah with his arm around her waist. I could see the glow on both their faces. Maybe from seeing us, but more likely because they were in love.

'Hi,' Mac and I called together, while they called out, 'Hello' at the same time. We all burst into laughter. It was such a relief from the tension of the past.

It wasn't until the evening when the children were in bed that we could talk about John.

'I am sad,' Jenny confessed. 'But I'm also relieved. No more running away. We can have a proper life.' She looked into Jed's eyes as he put his arm around her shoulders, looking deeply into her eyes, squeezing her gently.

'Good for me, too,' he said, looking across at us. 'I want to marry your daughter. She's the one for me and I'll look after her forever.'

I couldn't hold back a broad smile.

'Have you told the children about their dad?' Mac asked Jenny, choosing not to acknowledge Jed's comment until he'd heard from Jenny on this sensitive subject.

Jenny shook her head. 'Not yet. We'll tell them after you've left for home.'

Three days later Jenny received a letter with a police logo on the envelope giving advice about the coroner's report. Jenny read it out to everyone.

'Dear Madam,

The inquest into the death of Mr John Stanford will be held on Monday 10th February. If you wish to be present to hear the coronial finding you may attend the Manly Court 2 at 10am.'

'I don't want to go but you can if you want to, Dad.'

Mac thought about it. 'I wouldn't mind going. I want to hear the verdict and be sure that we don't find ourselves involved in a murder case.'

Very early the next morning we set off for home. We had relaxed and enjoyed the company of our daughter and grandchildren, as well as her new almost-fiancé. But now we were feeling down to earth again. It was a quiet trip home as we concentrated on our own thoughts.

……………..

On Monday 10th we were outside Manly Court ten minutes before 10am. A clutch of police we recognised – Sgt Ronson, Constable Bailey and Detective Rogers – were also there chatting with colleagues. They didn't acknowledge us at all. We all trooped in just before 10am and waited for the judge.

Mac and I had chosen to sit at the back because we didn't want to be seen.

The first person called to the stand was a doctor. He was an older man with a beard and wisps of hair combed over his bald head. He wore a shirt and tie, brown trousers and a tweed coat.

This was not an ordinary court, we knew, where lawyers asked questions. In this court the judge asked his own questions.

'Please advise the court of what you found when you attended the property in Narrabeen?'

'At 6am on Wednesday 27th I attended a call from Collaroy Police Station. I found a fully submerged man in the bath. On later examination I was able to determine that he had recently been using marijuana and his blood alcohol level was five times higher than the legal limit.'

The coroner interrupted there. 'Can you state that the drugs and alcohol caused him to fall asleep in the bath and drown?'

'Yes. Normally, a person with this much alcohol in their system will still wake up when water reaches their nose and mouth and prevents them from breathing.

However, with the addition of marijuana, a person's reflexes are impaired and they would not necessarily wake from the water, but may actually believe they are in a warm and cosy state. My diagnosis is that he drowned in the bath when he did not wake as the water rose to his nose and mouth.'

I sat there stunned. They were saying that because he was all alone, he did not wake up when the water rose. I felt terrible. If only I had done something.

Over the previous few days, there had been plenty of time to think about what I could have done. I could have made a loud noise that would have woken him and then he would have struggled to sit up and wouldn't have drowned.

It had taken me a few days to come up with this idea and I possibly wouldn't have thought of it during the panic at the time, but that didn't help me at all.

How could I let someone die? How could I let my son-in-law die even if he had caused our family so much trouble? I slumped down in my seat.

The next person on the stand was the police first responder to the scene. He was the same officer who had come to our door the next day.

'I was called to the property by the next door shop owner who'd seen water cascading from loose boards in the bathroom. He was aware it was the bathroom because of the tiny windows that are prevalent in that style of home. The back door wasn't locked and water was pouring over the floor. I initiated entry to the property as I had concerns about the welfare of the owner. The bathroom door was ajar and I could see water running over the rim of the bath. There was an empty bottle of scotch, *Jack Daniels* by label, on the floor next to the head of the bath. On the ledge at the corner of the bath where there's a flat section for soap, stood a whiskey glass that was empty. I came closer to the bath and saw Mr John Stanford lying, submerged. He wasn't breathing. I turned off the taps, and pulled Mr Stanford's head up to the air to breathe. This may have changed the scene of the event, but I needed to make sure that he couldn't be resuscitated. Unfortunately he was a grey colour and showed signs of purple around his mouth and eyes. His body was also beginning to bloat badly. I then phoned the doctor and the team to come to my assistance and perform their duties upon a corpse with an unknown cause of death.'

I'd been sitting in a state of panic for all this time. *Should I go to the police and confess that I was there and hadn't helped? Could I really live with this terror forever?*

Though my mind was in a state of confusion, I still managed to hear some of the words that the officer had said. It felt as if my mind had been split in two. He'd said that there was an empty glass of whiskey on the bath ledge.

I closed my eyes and recalled what I'd seen through the door that night.

John was in the kitchen before going into the bathroom. I'd heard the clink of glass on glass as he filled a glass from a bottle. Then I peered through the gap in the half-open door frame. I saw him place on the bathroom floor the almost-full bottle of whiskey that he'd brought in with him from the kitchen. I also saw him place the full to brimming glass of whiskey on the ledge before he climbed into the bath. Then I saw him fall asleep without having a drop. The full whiskey glass and bottle were still there when I crept out.

I shook my head and hoped that I'd heard correctly. Fortunately for me the coroner asked a few questions about the statement.

'So there was an empty bottle of whiskey by the bath and an empty whiskey glass on the bath shelf indicating that he'd been drinking in the bath?'

The officer nodded and said, 'Yes. We also found a plastic bag in the bedroom with a few grams of marijuana still inside. This supports the testament of the doctor that the man had also taken some drugs before moving to the bathroom.'

I didn't hear any more. I was off the hook.

Yes, I'd seen a full glass and nearly full bottle of whiskey. This could only mean that John had woken up after I left, and had poured himself several more glasses of whiskey, enough that the bottle was empty when the police arrived. It could only mean that he was alive when I left. I couldn't have done anything to save him as I wasn't anywhere near him when he finished the whiskey and fell asleep.

No one could have helped him!

My mind came back to the courthouse and the judge who was just pronouncing his verdict.

Misadventure! I had never before heard such a wonderful word.

Mac and I gave each other a steady stare. Mac believed that *karma* had caught up with John and we were safe. I was aware that this was a simplistic interpretation of *karma*, but I could see the relief on his face that we were not being charged with murder, and that's all that counted. He could also see the relief on my face, even though he would never know why I was so relieved.

Mac squeezed my hand, and as the judge said his final words and closed the case, we walked hand-in-hand out of the courtroom and into the sunlight of Manly Corso.

The sun was bright. The glimpse we caught of harbour at the ferry wharf was turquoise blue with tiny white wavelets lapping the old ferry that was birthed there. The people passing by looked happy and purposeful.

Everything seemed better, brighter, than it had before.

Angela's Anorexia:
The story
of my mother

A son's story of the debilitating illness, anorexia nervosa, that his single mother suffered from throughout his childhood. The mother and son formed a close bond and the boy's description of their life together is filled with both joy and sadness. A true story showing the boy's experience of growing up fast in Australia and New Zealand, caring for his mother while coming to understand her sickness and his need to develop an independent spirit early on.

Damian Cooper has written a straightforward, honest and loving account of his boyhood, set against a poignant parallel story of his mother's excessive focus on body image, food, diet and exercise.

Category: SELF-HELP/EATING DISORDERS AND BODY IMAGE

ARCO:
the legend
of the blue vortex

An exciting new story from first-time novelist, **Ferdinando Manzo**, ARCO explores man's battle with the sea in an attempt to seek solace.

The story is set in two different eras: on the high seas among ancient pirates and in contemporary Europe ravaged by war. The legend of the blue vortex – a door into another world – is the central focus of both periods.

An adventure story, it also raises philosophical questions about love and the purpose of life.

Category: FICTION MAGICAL REALISM/ROMANCE/FANTASY

Burma My Mother
And Why I Had To Leave

Myanmar's future is informed by its past - and BURMA MY MOTHER tells it like it is.

A valuable story of living through good times and plenty of bad in Burma, now known as Myanmar, before an escape to a new life of freedom.

Author **Sao Khemawadee Mangrai**'s husband, Hom, was imprisoned for 5 years, and his father was shot and killed sitting alongside independence leader, General Aung San, when he was assassinated.

Khemawadee grew up in a Shan state in the north-east of Myanmar, previously known as Burma, and now lives in Sydney. Her sad memories are also infused by the beauty of the country and the grace of Myanmar's Buddhist culture.

Category: MEMOIR

Drenched
by the Sun

I, who prophesy
by reading the stars and the wind,
now think of that country ...

Syam Sudhakar 'has an eye for the strange and the uncanny and a way of building translucent metaphors,' according to leading South Indian poet, K. Satchidanandan.

An award-winning poet who writes in English and Malayalam, Sudhakar is based in Kerala, teaching and researching Indian poetry.

Category: POEMS

Night Road to Life

Themes of the sea and the emotions, particularly the deeply felt joys and melancholies experienced by men, are a touchstone of NIGHT ROAD TO LIFE.

Ferdinando Manzo's thoughts are not bound to fluidity; they fly to the greatest heights of exhilaration in poems such as, *The sky above us*, which displays 'a mantle of stars that burns in my heart' and in the evocative lines of *Eclipse*: 'the moon rose, bright between the eyelids of the night'. Even the constellation Andromeda is given due recognition, breaking her chains and ready for revenge, before another poem *The voice of the universe* explores 'a hidden legend as far away as waves in outer space'.

A distinctive quality of this collection of poems is its musicality – the sounds of words carefully chosen, and their rhythms. The pleasing effect of the sensuality of sounds, ranging from gentleness to the drama of sex, is in tune with the gamut of human emotion.

Category: POEMS

Road to Rishi Konda

'ROAD TO RISHI KONDA' by **Geetha Waters** is a memoir of insight and charm, with a serious educational purpose. The author recalls delightful and stimulating stories from her childhood to throw light on the work of the philosopher J. Krishnamurti as a revolutionary 20th century educator.

At once fascinating and enchanting, Geetha Waters' stories centre on a girl growing up in Kerala and Andhra Pradesh in the '60s and '70s.

These youthful tales are underpinned by Geetha's deep understanding of childhood education, based both on her academic studies and in practice in her daily life as a mother and childcare professional.

Written from a child's perspective, the tales of awakening to life offer the reader an opportunity to appreciate how all children learn, as they draw on a deep well of curiosity that needs to be respected.

Category: BIOGRAPHY & AUTOBIOGRAPHY
PERSONAL MEMOIRS/EDUCATORS

Road
to Mandalay
Less Travelled

The Road to Mandalay

Less Travelled

Ingrid Raj

'The Road to Mandalay Less Travelled' by **Ingrid Raj** provides research on a selection of Anglo-Burmese writing published from the period of British rule in Burma up until 2007.

What Raj shares with us in this study is the knowledge she gained about the value of social resistance achieved through writing. Both fiction and non-fiction texts are included in arguing a case that these might be viewed as tools of often ambivalent resistance against oppressive regimes, both local and colonial.Her research deserves a wider readership than was initially provided, and to this aim Sydney School of Arts & Humanities presents the work as its first publication in this new category of Essays & Theses.

We hope that specialist researchers as well as members of the general reading public take this opportunity to learn more about the culture of the people of Myanmar through their unique approach to storytelling, based largely on their religious understanding, their rich store of folk legend and their chequered history.

Category: MEMOIRS/LITERATURE/BURMA-HISTORY

Jiddu Krishnamurti World Philosopher
Revised Edition

The life of the 20th-century philosopher Jiddu Krishnamurti was truly astonishing. As this new updated edition shows, people from all over the world would gather to hear him speak the wisdom of the ages.

Biographer **Christine (CV) Williams** carried out research over a period of four years to write this ebook account of Krishnamurti's life. She studied his major archive of personal correspondence and talks, and interviewed people who knew him intimately.

Krishna was born into poverty in a South Indian village, before being adopted by a wealthy English public figure, Annie Besant. As an adult he settled in California, travelling to India and England every year to give public lectures that inspired spiritual seekers beyond any single religion.

Category: BIOGRAPHY